An
ALFRED HITCHCOCK
Mystery

THE
VERTIGO
MURDERS

J. MADISON DAVIS published his first novel, *The Murder of Frau Schutz*, in 1988. It was voted one of the five Best First mysteries by the Mystery Writers of America and received an Edgar Allen Poe Scroll. His next book was *White Rook,* and his third, *Bloody Marko,* was called "superb" by the *New York Times.* His novel *Red Knight* continued the characters of *White Rook* and was a finalist for the Oklahoma Book Award for best novel by an Oklahoma writer. His most recent novel is *And the Angels Sing,* also nominated for the Oklahoma Book Award.

He has also published several nonfiction books, including *Dick Francis, Conversations with Robertson Davies, Stanislaw Lem: A Reader's Guide,* and *Critical Essays on Edward Albee* (with Philip C. Kolin). His *Shakespeare Name Dictionary* (with A. Daniel Frankforter) was published in 1995. *Murderous Schemes,* an anthology of mystery stories edited with Donald Westlake, was published by Oxford University Press in 1996 and called "the best book of its kind this year" by the *Wall Street Journal.*

Davis was elected president of the North American Branch of the International Association of Crime Writers in 1993 and reelected in 1995. He has served as the senior professor in the Professional Writing Program for the University of Oklahoma's H.H. Herbert School of Journalism since 1991.

THE VERTIGO MURDERS

AN
ALFRED HITCHCOCK
MYSTERY

J. MADISON DAVIS

ibooks
new york
www.ibooksinc.com

DISTRIBUTED BY SIMON & SCHUSTER

An Original Publication of ibooks, inc.

Pocket Books, a division of Simon & Schuster, Inc.
1230 Avenue of the Americas, New York, NY 10020

ibooks, inc.
24 West 25th Street
New York, NY 10010

The ibooks World Wide Web Site Address is:
http://www.ibooksinc.com

ISBN 0-7434-0728-8
First Pocket Books printing October 2000
10 9 8 7 6 5 4 3 2 1

Cover photograph copyright © Hulton-Deutsch Collection/Corbis
Cover photograph coloring by Richie Fahey
Cover design by Mike Rivilis
Typesetting by Wildside Press

Printed in the U.S.A.

Share your thoughts about *The Vertigo Murders*
and other ibooks titles in the new ibooks virtual
reading group at www.ibooksinc.com

For Mrs. Blue:
good cook,
wise advisor,
and perfect mother

THE
VERTIGO
MURDERS

CHAPTER
ONE

It all started out as a way of making a little extra after going Pink.

Going Pink isn't exactly like working. You wander around the floor of the warehouse or whatever it is you're supposed to protect, smoke cigarettes, listen to the radio, read the papers front to back, sneak a drink now and again, and think about all those other people out there. They're asleep, dreaming of whatever. You're awake, dreaming of being one of them.

The particular warehouse I was guarding was the size of an airline hanger. Its contents were cars, racks of them on steel tiers, along with a dozen stagecoaches and four tanks. There were Buicks, Chevys, Rolls Royces, Packards, and Model Ts. There were Duesenbergs and Willys Jeeps. I knew there was even a Stanley Steamer under one of the tarps, though I had been told I was absolutely, never, ever, to nose around, sit in the cars, nothing. The touch of a loser like me, I supposed, could taint the magic. Charlie Chaplin and Jean Harlow and Theda Bara and John Gilbert and John Wayne and god knows who had been filmed in these cars. There was a rumor the studio was going to have to auction off the whole collection to make ends meet.

Pinks are as common as bad actors in Babylon, but they're further down the feeding chain, even below the junk they protect. They're even lower than a real cop, which I had been until I decked a phony cowboy star named Smoky Tex Grady. He was drunkenly trying to filet me with a Jim Bowie-sized letter opener.

His nose was a bit rearranged by the encounter. Afterwards he kind of looked like somebody in a Black-and-Blue Period Picasso.

It messed up the shooting of a major picture, and that messed me up, though not as much as the phony cowboy had messed up his girlfriend. She got a big payoff and much sympathy for her "automobile accident." I got canned, no payoff, and no sympathy. And I got to wear the fourth uniform of my life, the one that got the least respect after my 82nd Airborne, my Boy Scout, and my LAPD uniforms.

I had been listening to the steel racks creaking at the temperature changes as the night crawled on for about six weeks. My relief showed up at five—on time for a change—and I stepped out into a vicious daybreak. My eyes watered so much I didn't immediately notice the cream-colored convertible Olds behind my coupe.

"You're Detective Slattery. Am I right?" The man behind the wheel wore a seersucker suit and a broad-brimmed panama. He was lighting a cigarette at the end of a long holder.

"Wrong," I said. "Will you move your car?"

"I was told Detective Slattery worked here."

"Wrong," I said again, my eyes gradually adjusting. He didn't look like a process server, I thought, and anyway why would the phony cowboy sue me? Whatever he was, he wasn't muscle.

"Is he inside?"

"Look," I said, "the name's Slattery, and if I was still a detective I wouldn't be dressed like a rent-a-cop, would I? Now are you going to move that car or am I going to back into it?"

The man twitched his pencil mustache. "Aw, now, don't be a sorehead. There's a grand or more in it for you."

"In it for me how?"

"It's a consulting job."

"Consulting on what?"

"Security."

I glanced up the mountain toward the "Hollywood" sign. "Look, I don't play twenty questions. Move the vehicle and let me go home to bed."

I began to round the rear of the car.

"Listen, buddy, there's nothing hinky about this." He plucked a business card off the dashboard and offered it, first to his right, and then as I moved past the trunk, to his left. "I'm Sig Fairfax. I'm in the publicity business, but I was asked to find you."

"Publicity? I don't need any publicity."

"Naw, naw, buddy. It's like this. Somebody important needs to talk with someone about security. So this person asked an acquaintance who'd be a good choice, and this acquaintance (of the important guy) said you might be interested, seeing as how you used to be a detective."

"Who are these people?"

"I don't know."

"Who contacted you?"

"Herbert Coleman's office."

"Am I supposed to know him?"

Fairfax struck a pose. "He's an associate producer at Paramount. He—"

"Well, ta ti tah, buddy. Move your car."

He looked bewildered. "Aw, come on. He got a recommendation from Captain Greene. The captain said you was one of the best detectives he ever had. He said he didn't know why you didn't go up to Frisco or New York."

"Yeah, well, the captain didn't do a helluva lot to keep me on the force, did he?"

When the studios barked, the whole chain of command in the city shivered until they could offer up a goat. That was me, this time.

"Move the car," I repeated.

"Suit yourself," said Fairfax, "but you get a grand for just talking to this person. Whether you take the job or not. It's just talk."

Talk is cheap, I thought, usually a lot cheaper than a grand. I was suspicious, but my interest was piqued.

"So, who is this important person?"

"Can't say."

"Can't?" I leaned over him like I was trying to force out a confession. Old habits.

"Literally, buddy, 'can't.'" He cringed slightly. "I don't know who it is. But this is the address." He had written it on the back of his card. "He—or it might be a she—wants to see you this morning, right away. You get a grand for just hearing him or her out."

The address was in a very good neighborhood. Bellagio Road in Bel Air. A grand wouldn't mean much to the people who lived in that neighborhood. "I'll think about it," I said, pocketing the card.

"No skin off my nose," he said, pulling away. "I delivered the message."

I did think about it. There were a thousand good reasons to go, but there might also be some very good reasons not to. It was still only about a month after I edited Smoky Tex Grady's face. He seemed stupid enough to hire a couple of stuntmen to grind me into sausage. But in Bel Air? Why not just pound me here?

At first, I set out for my apartment. I don't know why I changed my mind. Something about the left turn made me think it ought to be a U.

CHAPTER TWO

I followed Sunset Boulevard west to Bel Air and Bellagio Road. It was just about six when I passed the front of the address Fairfax had given me. The mansions along the winding road had tropical plants and a green lawn that looked as comfortable as your mother's bosom.

The house I wanted was nearly at the end of a loop up against the Bel Air Country Club golf course. I went further around past the house, pulled over, and looked back, waiting ten minutes to see if anyone was expecting me. No one poked his head out to see why I had passed without stopping.

I checked that my rent-a-cop sidearm was loaded, then got my ankle piece out of the glove compartment and strapped it on. If Smoky Tex Grady was behind all this, he'd find out what a shoot-out was really about.

I drove back, pulled up the driveway, and once again eyed the property. When I rang the doorbell, the peephole blinked. I felt silly in my uniform.

A woman wearing an old-fashioned maid's uniform peered out.

"Chess Slattery," I said. "Sig Fairfax gave me a card—" I fumbled in my pocket. "It's—"

"Come in," said the woman. "You're expected." She led me towards the back. As we passed the staircase, I caught a glimpse of an older woman in a dressing gown passing the upper landing. The maid tapped on a heavy door and opened it without waiting for an answer.

"Mr. Hitchcock will see you now," she said.

The Mr. Hitchcock? Alfred Hitchcock?"

There are a lot of Hitchcocks in the world, I suppose. But only one in Hollywood. Alfred Hitchcock. The master of suspense.

He was sitting at a heavy desk, a script spread out in front of him. There were neat bookshelves behind him with the kind of books that look like props hiding a wall safe. An expensive oriental rug covered the floor. A large window revealed that the house sat with its back to the Bel Air Country Club. A duffer was putting on the eighteenth hole. Another man in golf clothes, all plaid and silly, held the flag and watched his partner make a three-footer. He wasn't a happy man.

Hitchcock smoothed the script pages flat and rocked back in his chair, lacing his fingers across his belly.

"Good morning," he said.

I blinked. I had met my share of movie stars, men who

looked better than their wax statues in Madame Tussaud's, women whose wink could send you to forty thousand feet and suck the oxygen out of your lungs. But this was six in the morning in far too weird circumstances, a real Hitchcock moment.

"You're Alfred Hitchcock," I stammered.

"Ummm, yes," he said, "and you are Mr. Slattery?"

"I think so. I'm beginning to think I could wake up and find out I'm President Eisenhower."

"You may," said Hitchcock, "but I should be very disappointed to be a figment of your imagination."

I didn't know what to say. "I like your movies, and your show, too. The commercial things, those 'our sponsor' things you do–"

He looked irritated and diffidently backhanded a wave at a wing-backed chair. "Please take a seat, Mr. Slattery. A car will be coming to take me to the studio in about fifteen minutes."

"Sure," I said, "sure."

"I am led to understand that you are late of the police department."

I shrugged. "I poked the wrong guy."

"So I understand. I do not know Smoky Tex, myself–" Hitchcock rolled the phony cowboy's name around his mouth like an overly tart lemon drop "–nor do I care to, but there is a considerable body of opinion that the cowpoke had earned much more than a poke."

"It wasn't the smartest thing I ever done."

He turned his chair slightly and looked down his nose at me. "Well, all that aside, I asked you here to make you a proposition. You may accept it or reject it as you wish, and I will pay you for your time in coming here."

"If I'm interested, we'll talk about money. I don't want to be paid for nothing."

"There is no obligation."

"There is always an obligation where money is concerned," I said. The tiniest bit of wry amusement played about his lips.

"I am told you are an honest man, Mr. Slattery, and one who can keep his counsels."

"Somebody's been spreading vicious rumors," I said.

"I had a few discreet inquiries made by my associate producer Herbert Coleman. Captain Greene suggested you are a good man for what I have in mind."

"This guy Fairfax said something about security."

"Fairfax is in the publicity department. Lower rungs. He is assigned to run some errands for us. Like many employees in this business, he gets in the way. I prefer to keep him distracted. I had Mr. Coleman telephone him with Captain Greene's information about where to find you."

"It sounds complicated."

"A studio," said Hitchcock, "is more Byzantine than Byzantium. Fairfax will likely sell a tip to one of the sleazier papers that Herbert and I are hiring you as an expert on police procedure. Once the story is about, no one will believe you if you deny it."

"Hooray for Hollywood."

"Precisely. The story will keep others confused about what your particular duties are."

"You're a sneaky guy."

He blinked. "I have spent many years learning what people are likely to believe."

He turned his chair again and moved a novel. Under it was a folded newspaper. "From now on, what we say must be in confidence."

"You're the boss."

His director's eyes dissected me for several seconds. He was considering what would happen if I were as untrustworthy as the usual moke.

"It doesn't leave the room," I said more seriously.

He made his decision and shoved the newspaper toward me. The story on top I had been reading earlier, in the middle of the night. "Are you familiar with the Baby Lowen case?"

On the left margin was a picture of two men in ill-fitting suits. Their arms were stiff at their sides, as if they had been zapped by a raygun from the planet Zyniac, but they were the true spacemen in L. A. The father's hat sat low on his head, touching his ears. Magnified by his thick specs, Edgar Lowen's wide eyes looked like undercooked fried eggs. He was looking toward the girl's fiancé, Raymond Cruikshank, whose head was lowered. The brim of his fedora covered everything but his jaw, as if he had broken down just as the photo was snapped. He was one of those country lummoxes who would only look normal in overalls. His hands hung like two hams in a curing shed. The two of them had come, said the cutline, to take Baby Lowen's body home to the town she'd grown up in. Another of those moments desecrated by gawking news cameras.

Baby Lowen was the blonde whose picture was on the right. Her face was round, the inspiration for her nickname, I supposed. Her lips were thick and her eyes had a heavy-lidded, anything-but-baby look. *I learned a lot down on the farm,* they seemed to say, *but a lot more since I left.*

She'd learned a lot more than she counted on, I thought.

"All I know about her is what I read in the papers. Of course you read a lot of papers going Pink."

"Excuse me?"

"Pinkerton. It means working security. Night watchman. It's not really *the* Pinkerton agency, but that's what we call the job. There's nothing much to do but read papers."

"'Going Pink,'" he said, as if making a mental note. "So you are aware of Baby Lowen?"

I explained that what I knew was only what anybody who'd read all of the papers front to back would know. That kind of thing always worked for Sherlock Holmes, but having been a cop I wasn't as optimistic the papers printed anything like the truth.

As far as the papers went, it should have been a "Dog Bites Man" story. Christina Marie, AKA "Baby," Lowen was just another bleach job who had come from the Midwest intent on becoming the next Marilyn Monroe. She'd knocked around town for about two years, getting a job in a drug store, getting her nickname, getting listed as an extra, getting plenty of the usual worthless advice, probably getting laid in return for the advice—in other words, getting nowhere.

If she hadn't gotten murdered in a particularly nasty way, nobody would have cared.

The last person to see her alive was a coffee jockey at an all-night diner. He noticed she'd looked upset. He saw her put makeup on the angle of her jaw to try to cover up a fresh bruise. She left there around 3 a.m. on Thursday, October 17.

They figured she was murdered that morning and was dumped sometime after the bank closed on Thursday afternoon. What was left of her was found on Friday morning in the space between two trash bins behind a Bank of Pasadena branch downtown.

The details were ugly, if you could believe what you read. Her throat had been slit and her torso split open from her groin to her collarbone. It took three days to figure out who she was. The rats had been at her.

"Like I said, I only know what I read in the papers," I answered. "Sounds like one of those psycho killings."

"Psycho," mused Hitchcock.

"Like the Ripper."

"The lodger seems to return every year," he sighed. "She is being compared to the Black Dahlia."

"That stuff sells papers."

"The Sig Fairfaxes of the world," he sneered.

"So, what have I got to do with this?"

Hitchcock thought for several seconds. I could hear the air whistling through his nose. He finally seemed to resolve whatever he was considering and extended one hand out on the desk. "I would like you to investigate it for me."

"The Baby Lowen murder? That's a cop thing. I'm not a detective anymore, Mr. Hitchcock. I got the boot."

"You have the skills and you know policemen. One of my best qualities as a boy was that I never wanted to be a policeman, so now I rely on others. The captain assured my colleague that you are scrupulously honest."

"I don't understand."

"You are to take what information I give you and whatever you uncover on your own and look into it. Whatever you find out you will report only to me."

"No, I meant does Captain Greene know what you want me to do?"

"I did not tell Mr. Coleman very much. So I can assure you he likely said even less to Captain Greene. I will, of course, keep the police fully informed if we come up with anything useful. However, under no circumstances is my involvement in this to be bruited about. Is that clear?"

"Complete secrecy, then." I leaned forward. "So exactly what do you mean by your involvement?"

"My interest, then."

"So what is your interest in this? A movie? If you want to trust me, I have to be able to trust you."

A rap at the door interrupted. The woman I had spotted on the landing stuck her head in.

"This is my wife, Mrs. Hitchcock," he said quickly. I had never thought about his being married. It was that common thing of the television personality not matching the real person. It was like thinking of Joe Friday's wife or even Rin Tin Tin. "This is Mr. Slattery."

"Pleased to meet you," she said. "Hitch, the limousine is here."

"Thank you," he said. "I'll be just a minute."

She left.

"You were asking what my interest is. It is not a movie. I'm not on the whole very interested in true stories. My only one, *The Wrong Man,* did rather badly."

"What is it, then?" Maybe it was Alma's sticking her head in the door that made me think perhaps he had known Baby Lowen. He was a real man, not someone created by a writer. He had a wife, he had normal desires—or at least some kind of desires. Perhaps he had known Baby Lowen too well. Stranger things went on in Hollywood. Much stranger.

"The police assume she was murdered early Thursday morning or possibly early Thursday afternoon," he said.

"They said something about the condition of the body. They look at things like rigor and so forth." This was all probably familiar to him, so I did not go on.

Hitchcock closed up the script and gathered some notes he had been making. He looked me in the eye. "I know she was alive on Thursday evening."

"How do you know that?"

"She had trespassed on the golf course."

"Excuse me?"

He twitched his head towards the window. "She had trespassed on the golf course."

"What do you mean?"

He glared at me. "I had just returned from a difficult day shooting a script called *From Among the Dead,* based on a French novel called *D'Entre les Morts.* If I have my way—which I shall—the film will be retitled *Vertigo.*"

"*Vertigo?*"

"It means a sensation of dizziness. In today's work, Jimmy Stewart visits his old friend and hears about the problem with the wife. Tom mispronounced 'Ernie's' several times."

"I like Jimmy Stewart," I said. I must have looked confused. A sensation of dizziness.

"We have just finished sixteen days of shooting in San Francisco. The studio is still pushing me to do something called *Flamingo Feather,* and we haven't agreed on what to call the new film. All this is neither here nor there to you, of course.

"The point is, I looked out the window. It was a nice evening. A blonde girl caught my eye. She was crossing the fairway in this direction. I assume she got past the golf course security. Two policemen came towards her from the rough, grabbed her by the arms, and dragged her away. She struggled. I could hear her shouting that it was 'okay,' that she knew me. She pointed at the house here and said she knew me. I did not know her at all, and don't believe any of them saw me. They hefted her by the arms and carted her away, into the shrubbery."

"That's odd," I said.

"Not when you're Alfred Hitchcock. I am frequently buttonholed by confused people who imagine they know me well in some otherworldly manner. It was not until the murdered girl was identified several days later and her photograph appeared in the weekend newspapers that I knew she was the same woman who had been arrested right there."

I walked to the window and peered out. The eighteenth hole was lovely. The rough on the opposite side was quite a distance. I bumped a box of broken glass with my foot.

"They often break the window," he said.

I must have given him a curious look.

"We call the clubhouse and they immediately send a glazier. It was broken last Friday."

Time to move, I thought. "How do you know it was the same woman?"

His nostrils flared. "My profession. I am better at faces than even you. I promise you."

"I didn't mean to imply anything, but I thought maybe you might have been mistaken. Newspaper photos are—"

"She was the same woman, Mr. Slattery."

I nodded. "Did you talk to Captain Greene, or get this guy Coleman to ask who picked her up?"

"No one other than Alma knows that I saw her."

"And you'd recognize the difference between police costumes and actual uniforms?"

His eyebrows lowered.

"I was just thinking out loud. This is the movie capital of the world. I had to ask."

"That is your responsibility," said Hitchcock.

I realized he assumed I had taken the job. I realized also that I had. I had just joined the infrequently honorable order of the private eye.

"Can you describe these cops?"

Hitchcock lifted his blotter and shoved a sheet of artist's sketch paper at me. On it were three pencil drawings. They were much more shadowy and impressionistic than the usual police renderings. My expression must have given away my surprise.

"By my hand," he said. "I apologize."

"No," I said. "They're excellent." I immediately recognized Baby Lowen from her newspaper photos. Her lips were full and sensual. Her eyes stared out as if you were the only man in the world. His drawing made her much more alluring than her newspaper photograph.

I studied the faces of the two cops for several seconds. The one looked a little familiar, but I couldn't place him. The other rang no bells.

"One other thing," said Hitchcock. "We will need a photograph of Baby Lowen which clearly shows her right ear."

"Huh? Why? The crime scene or the autopsy photos might show her right ear."

"I have my doubts," he said, standing, "but, if they do, there is yet another amusement for us." Taking a handkerchief from his coat pocket, he reached behind a stack of books on the shelf behind him. He brought out a box about four inches square. It was loosely wrapped in brown paper. When he lifted off the box's lid, inside there was a milk-glass Pond's cold cream jar.

"This anonymous gift," he said, "was delivered to my office at the studio on Friday. In it is a woman's right ear."

CHAPTER
THREE

CHAPTER
THREE

Hitchcock told me to wait inside until the limousine had left. Mrs. Hitchcock offered me coffee, which I accepted, and told me to call her Alma. She apologized, said something about promising Pat, her daughter, to check on the sprinklers, and left the house herself. The maid served the coffee to me in paper-thin china on the back veranda. I noticed someone had collected golf balls in a bucket and that there was one in the flowerpot and another nestled in the branches of a low hedge. I positioned myself under the umbrella. I had the feeling the maid was watching me the whole time from behind a curtain, but I never caught her.

The edginess I felt had something to do with the men in silly clothes whacking balls in my general direction, but was more from lack of sleep. On the other hand, I was anything but sleepy. My mind raced at all that had happened. I couldn't bring myself to believe Hitchcock was telling me the whole story. The girl appears out his back window hours *after* she has been slaughtered? He doesn't know anything about her, yet someone sends her ear to him?

If it was Baby Lowen's ear.

It was an ear all right, floating in the Pond's jar in some kind of clear vinegary liquid. The lobe appeared to have a puncture hole, so it was the ear either of a woman or a pirate. Baby Lowen hadn't been a pirate, as far as I knew, but she had definitely been a woman. That didn't mean it was *her* ear, however.

On the wrapper there was nothing but the words, "For Alfred Hitchcock," in block letters. Inside the jar lid, however, crude words had been scratched into the tin. The exposed metal had already begun to rust from the liquid that was pickling the ear. The lettering inside the lid resembled the lettering on the paper, but that probably meant nothing.

"YOUR SHARE," it said. Of Baby Lowen?

My imagination ran a bit. Guy orders a hit. The hit men dress as cops, like it's St. Valentine's Day again. They prove they've done the job by sending the ear. To establish an alibi, the guy who hired them then hires an ex-cop to track him down? That would out-Hitchcock Hitchcock. The hit men got their addresses confused? Maybe they sent it thinking Hitchcock would tell the police, then it would be in the newspapers, and the guy who hired them would know —

This was turning as nuts as a Charlie Chan episode. A little more Jack Webb and Ben Alexander was in order.

"Just the facts, ma'am," I reminded myself. But how to go about getting them?

I decided my rent-a-cop uniform was a little too humiliating to visit the station house, but by the time I'd showered and put on my gray suit, I'd begun to feel more raggedy than Andy. I tanked up on a greasy breakfast in a diner, which woke me up by setting fire to my guts, then wandered to the police station to see what I could squeeze out of my former colleagues.

"Chester," said Sergeant Everson, as I stepped through the low gate, "what are you doing back here, civilian? You ain't supposed to be in here."

"Old times," I said. "How's business?"

"Win a few, lose a few." He scratched his bald head. "Seriously, you ain't supposed to be in here past the rail. I could get in trouble for talking to you."

"The movie people are that pissed off?"

"The asshole's broken nose cost them about half a million, I hear."

"They ought to be grateful. I saved them the million they would have lost making another Smoky Tex turkey."

Everson laughed. "I hear you got him good."

"He's a pansy," I said. "Say, you got any coffee? I'm lonely for the jailhouse joe."

"You're a sick man, Slattery. You sure Smoky Tex didn't give you a concussion? Come on, then. If you can drink crude oil, I can pump it."

We stepped into the closet that had been converted into the coffee room. Everson wiped the rim of a cracked, heavy cup with his thumb and forefinger, then poured the black liquid. I wondered if it was the cup he had resorted to in beating down the hophead who had busted up the squad room last June.

I tried to sound casual. "Say, Ev, you heard anything about the Baby Lowen killing?"

"Heard plenty," he said. "What's it to you?"

"Just curious. One of the guys at the warehouse said he thought he saw her on the Thursday night before they found the body."

"Couldn'ta been her. She was dead by Thursday morning. They say 3 a.m. to 9 a.m."

"That's what I told him." I shrugged. I realized the oily coffee was throwing gas on the fire in my stomach. "How'd they know? Three to nine is a long time."

"It's one of those expert opinions. The coroner thought she had ripened up for at least twenty-four hours, so they wrote it down that way."

"She left the diner at three and the bankers get in at nine."

"Right."

"So she laid out there all day until they came back to work on Friday?"

"That's what they say. The manager says he didn't look behind the trash cans when he left on Thursday night."

"Maybe she wasn't there."

Everson twisted his lips and dropped his head. "I'm just telling you what the smart boys decided. I'm just a dumb cop. You ain't even that. What's your interest, Chester?"

"Nothing." I made a face. "Is it worse to you when a woman gets it?"

Everson paused a moment, then said, "The young ones is what gets me, girls or boys."

"Well, it's almost always somebody close. I'd sniff around her friends. Even the bank guy."

Everson slapped my back. "Kick a guy off the force and they start thinking they're Sherlock Holmes. The bank guy's clean, no connection to the broad. The girl didn't have many friends, but she made a lot of acquaintances."

"Hooking?"

"Not in the best professional tradition, but she probably had a few friends who wouldn't want their names in *Hollywood Tattletale.*"

"Big stars? Naw, they're all pure as the driven snow."

"And when has it snowed around here lately?" Everson moved to go back to work.

"Tell me this," I said. "Did anybody arrest a blonde up on the golf course in Bel Air on that Thursday?"

Everson looked at me curiously. "How would I know that?"

"It just sticks in my head. The guy at the warehouse golfs. He said he saw two cops dragging Baby Lowen off the Bel Air Country Club course that afternoon. I mean, if she was still alive late Thursday—"

"Oh, come on, Slattery, don't come around here with some bullshit rumor."

"It isn't a rumor. It's just between you, me, and the guy who told me. Do I look like a reporter?"

"Shit like that gets said and the next thing you know a shyster's throwing it back in your face just before the murderer waves bye-bye. This 'guy' of yours probably passed a movie set. How many bleached blondes you think are wandering around LA? Eight million?" Everson's face had turned red.

"Hey, Sarge, I wasn't—"

"Who is this 'guy' anyway?"

"He's just a guy who works at the warehouse. Fixes fancy cars."

"And what was a mechanic doing golfing up there?"

"Did you ever get a Rolls repaired? There was no cameraman or anything like a filming. He was sure it wasn't acting."

"Haven't you got anything better to do?" He pulled away. "Take a hike!" He pulled away and made for his desk.

I set down the station house coffee and shrugged.

My first shot at playing private eye hadn't gone all that smooth. Was Everson angry for the reason he said? Or was it there was more to this murder than he could say? Who were the "big stars" Baby Lowen was servicing?

I remembered it going a lot worse when I was first a police detective, however. I said what the hell and decided I'd take a run at Captain Greene. I went upstairs and found him with his back to his open door, grumbling into the phone. It gave me a chance to collect my thoughts.

"Well, yeah," he was saying, his wild eyebrows pumping. "I can put another patrol in that area, but where am I going to take it from? Jesus H. Mulligan! I got two cars down and four men who retired last month. That's what I keep telling you. Yeah. Well, explain it to him."

He pulled the receiver away from his ear and eyeballed it as if it were terminally stupid. He then sensed me over his shoulder.

"Slattery, what are you doing here? You got no business here."

"I wanted to drop by and thank you."

"For what? Being the guy to can you?"

"For lining me up for the security job with the studio. I was getting pretty tired of watching cars collect dust."

Greene fidgeted with the papers on his desk. "No big deal. It was pretty strange when the secretary said, 'Please hold for Paramount.' I thought it was a gag. The guy asked for someone who knew police procedures. He said he worked with Alfred Hitchcock. I thought that was a gag, too. What's the deal?"

"The big man wants to know things about fingerprints and evidence and stuff like that. Routine crap. Something about one of the television things. Nothing important."

"Hey, if it comes up, I could give them plenty of ideas."

I snapped my fingers and eased the door closed. "Listen, though, maybe you *could* help me out on something. It might get me in good with, you know, the bosses."

Greene looked suspicious.

"The Baby Lowen thing."

"Yes."

"I get the impression some people over there at Paramount are nervous about it."

"Like who?"

"I don't know for sure, yet. The girl was trying to break into movies is what I heard. She was willing to do what nice girls don't."

"Nice girls don't get into movies."

"So there are people afraid they might get dragged into this."

"There always are," scowled the captain. "If they'd learn to stay out of the submarine races, they wouldn't have to worry."

"Amen to that. Are you on to any of these racers?"

The captain stared at me for a minute. "A few. But I'm not talking. It doesn't matter where it comes from. It gets in the papers, I get the blame."

"Come on! You know I wouldn't work for the papers!"

"I know nothing of the kind, Chess. With all due respect, your once being a fellow officer and all."

"Thanks a whole hell of a lot."

He raised an eyebrow. "A guy gets kicked off the force, gets bitter—God knows. Nothing personal."

I thought about Everson downstairs. He might just tell Greene what I had asked about in the coffee room. "I understand. Let me open up a bit and you can tell me what you think. Could Baby Lowen have been arrested on Thursday afternoon?"

"For what? Being dead isn't illegal."

"How do you know she was dead by then? Based on what? The coroner's say so? That's just a guess. What's the difference? Has she got to be dead by before the bank opens?"

"An educated guess. He's seen his share of stiffs."

"So have you and I," I said.

Maybe I was being optimistic, but I thought I saw the captain's hard features soften a bit. We band of brothers.

He snatched a note pad. "Who and where?"

"A guy said he saw Baby Lowen being carried off the Bel Air golf course around eight on Saturday evening."

"Who's the guy?"

"I can't tell you."

"One of the big shots who belongs to the club, eh?"

"He didn't know her. He recognized her later from the picture in the papers."

"What do you mean by 'carried off'?"

"Not like a kidnapping," I said. "Like she was being arrested."

"Car number? Cops' names?"

I shook my head. "One was heavyset and had a wattle. The other had a big jaw. The description of the heavyset guy sounded kind of familiar, but I can't place him."

"Jesus H. Mulligan, Slattery. You're giving me nothing to go on," scowled Greene.

"But you can find out who was in the area maybe and ask them. Maybe they just took her out of the area and didn't file a report. She could have hooked up with the killer later."

"No cops of mine did this!" He tapped a folder on his desk and I realized it was the Lowen file. "This was a sick bastard."

"No, but you don't want rumors getting around. Maybe they're keeping quiet because she did them a favor, if you catch my drift."

Greene nodded. It wasn't only the stars who went to the submarine races. Cops have been known, on occasion, to get distracted by their torpedoes, too. "I'll look into it."

"I thought you might like to know. Once a cop, always a cop."

He chewed on the idea I was doing him a favor. "I appreciate it."

I took a deep breath. "Listen, have you got any pictures of Baby Lowen? Other than those in the papers?"

"Why?"

"I thought maybe the guy might change his mind if he saw a better picture of her. I figure he's mistaken."

"This is all we've got," said Greene. He flipped open the folder and shoved an eight by ten at me.

You couldn't recognize Baby Lowen's head from her close-up. You could barely recognize her as a human. There isn't much left when you cut away the nose, the lips, most of the skin, and the ears.

"This is one sick bastard," repeated Greene.

CHAPTER
FOUR

I pulled up to the gate at Paramount and asked to see Mr. Hitchcock. The guard asked if I was on the list. I told him I was sure I wasn't, but that I worked for Mr. Hitchcock and it was very important I see him. If he would just call down—

All of this worked about as well as Wheatena substituting for motor oil. After several arguments he just told me to go away. I left a message which I was sure would never reach the man.

I headed back to my apartment, thinking I'd catch up on a little shut-eye before trying his house around dinnertime. I was almost there when I thought of the *Herald*. I pulled into a gas station and called Freddy Mancik. Freddy had come to LA thinking he had a movie to write. The only work he ever got at a studio was serving as an extra in a couple of war pictures. During the war he had written for *Stars and Stripes,* so he changed his career goal to making studios execs terrified of what might appear in his gossip column.

He was always straight with me, but I had to make certain he didn't find out who I was working for or he'd make it into something. You never knew what, except it would begin with either "People in the know are saying . . ." or "The word on the street is . . ."

"Freddy," he answered.

"This is Slattery."

"Hey, finally going to give us the exclusive on decking Smoky Tex? Sixty bucks."

"No, Freddy, I—"

"Seventy-five, for old times' sake. I'll write it, you just say it's true. You don't have to do a thing."

"Freddy, keep your filthy money." He laughed, wheezing. "I just called to ask where you got the picture of Baby Lowen."

"AP. Why're you asking?"

"I was hoping you had more."

"Man, I'm looking, even though I'm not sure we can run them."

"What do you mean? The publisher got religion? He's clamping down on your sleaze? How will civilization survive?"

Freddy whistled. "Those kind of pictures would get us a jail cell."

"Nudies?"

"That's what I hear. She had a boyfriend photog. He did a portfolio for her she was circulating."

"The nudies?"

"Well, they weren't in her regular portfolio, but I'm trying to run down a calendar out of Chicago. What's your interest?"

"I'm trying to get a good head shot of her, one different from in the papers. It's to straighten up an ID that may be wrong."

"Are you telling me the murdered girl might not be Baby Lowen? Holy mackerel!"

"No. That's not it at all. A guy thought he saw her, but I think it was just somebody who resembled the AP Wirephoto."

I could almost hear Freddy thinking. He was wondering what my interest in this was. After all, I wasn't a police detective anymore. "Maybe you got something for me, Chess?"

"Nothing, really. Who was the boyfriend? Maybe I can help you run down the nudies."

"There's three hundred bucks in it for you if you do. And I mean it. We'll print 'em with just the head or fig leaves or something. I'll give you fifty for the calendar. The boyfriend's name is Leonardo Ventuno. His shop is at the bad end of Vine."

"Ventuno?" The name rang a bell. He advertised himself as "photographer to the stars," but he danced around the edges of the Cosa Nostra. He'd been charged with collecting protection money when I was a rookie cop, but while he was in the lockup, the witness disappeared. Later I heard he was in the eight-millimeter porno business, but nobody much cared if he was. For a lot of cops porn was good enough to shake a guy down, but not good enough to arrest him.

"I've been over there a dozen times this week, though, and the shop is never open. He doesn't answer his phones, either. If I had more time—"

"I'll do what I can."

"Thanks. I'll give you a hundred you give me the Smoky Tex story."

"No can do."

"What a thief! One and a quarter, then. Better take it before his girlfriend talks."

"She's bought off good and you know it. I'll get back to you on Ventuno."

It took me twenty minutes to get to the end of Vine. Ventuno's two-story shop looked like it had been closed for fifty years. Trash had blown into the doorway. The coating of dust on the windows made the faded photographs in the window look even more ancient. Two were of Mae Murray and Wallace Reid. Ventuno was far too young to have taken those. Reid had died from drugs in the twenties, an early victim of the movie set "doctor." Murray had quit in the 1930s, I think. There was a picture of Clark Gable I recognized. It was by Yousef Karsh. I'm sure Karsh didn't know his work was so well placed. I couldn't see anything else in the windows.

The flaking lettering on the door said "Photographer to the Stars," but should have said "Pornographic Purveyor to the Mob." Ventuno might have taken some pictures once in a while, but the shop looked like he was less of a photographer than even we on the force had imagined. I banged on the door for a while, but nothing stirred but dust. I slipped down the alley to the back.

Up on the second floor I could see a window open. I called up. "Hello? Anybody home?"

Nothing.

The back door was solid oak, with three iron bands holding it together. The keyhole, I noticed, had clean scratches around the opening from someone trying to get a key into it, which meant someone had been trying to get in within recent memory. Trash hadn't accumulated in the opening either, and I thought there were some tracks in the footpath going back to the alley gate.

I checked it out, but it was an alley like any other. Fences and trash cans. Ventuno probably came and went through the back, but where he had gone to at the moment was a big question. I thought about all the places a two-bit thug in pointy shoes might hang out. Half a dozen came easily to mind, but there was no use going to any of them until evening.

The shrill ring of a phone startled me. I had just walked under the open window. Probably Freddy trying to call Ventuno again, I thought. It rang ten times, then stopped.

I crossed the street and asked in the drug store if anybody had seen Ventuno lately. The pharmacist in the back just looked up, adjusted his tortoiseshell glasses, and shrugged. He didn't miss a stroke in counting his pills.

The girl at the lunch counter was wearing a sweater so tight it could have exploded and killed the two men eating apple pie. Hey, it worked for Lana Turner, right?

"Sometimes guys go in and out," she said, looking out the window. She didn't know who.

"If you notice anything, will you give me a call?" I

scribbled down my number and wrapped it in a five-dollar bill. She glanced to see if the pharmacist was watching, then winked. The two men at the counter had murder in their eyes.

I'd gotten a delicious wink out of running all around town, but that was about it. A fine private eye I was turning out to be. I went home to take a nap.

CHAPTER
FIVE

I slept as sound as Baby Lowen, but not quite as comfortable. Somehow my dreams got mixed up with those nightmares in *Spellbound*. Baby Lowen was skiing and Gregory Peck was shouting to keep her away from a tree. She hit the tree and was split in half and I woke up.

I reached Hitchcock's house about eight. He wasn't back from the studio yet. "He works a long day," I said.

"Of course," said Alma, as if it were the most obvious thing on earth.

She allowed me to wait in a sitting room, and the maid brought me a very English tray of tea with milk and some kind of pastries I figured were crumpets.

By nine-thirty I knew I wasn't going in to Pink anymore. It made no sense. I hadn't found out much of anything for

Hitchcock, but I was already thinking of myself as a private eye. I just couldn't bring myself to put on that awful uniform again. I phoned them I was quitting and they weren't too happy. Some other Pink would be working a double shift on time and a half—if they didn't figure out some way to screw him out of it.

Around ten-thirty Alma apologized, but she was going to bed. I offered to come back tomorrow, but she said these hours weren't unusual. I should make myself at home.

I tried to get interested in one of the books in the sitting room. There were a lot of mysteries, some of which I recognized, but most of which I figured were just good for a laugh. Dead vicars, cigarette ashes on the rug, train schedules, and untraceable poisons: that kind of thing. I began to pace and eventually drifted down to the great man's office.

Hesitating at the door, I listened. The house was utterly silent. I turned the knob and went in. I fumbled the desk lamp on. A script lay on the desk, perhaps the same I had seen that morning. There were several in a stack, however, and they all looked pretty much the same. I opened it and saw his notes to the writer. He wanted this shorter. This longer. There were sketches of the positions of certain shots, and even notations about the length of a shot. There were other notes I didn't understand at all. "Norman Lloyd?" asked one. "I know she will die for the role, but will she dye for it?"

I looked at my watch and it was nearing midnight. There are certain kinds of jobs, I thought, which make it very easy to arrange adultery. The traveling salesman, the hotel manager, and, yes, the cop. But for a director, well, not only could you be out at all hours with your wife none the wiser, but if you were an important director there were plenty of girls (and boys!) who were willing to do whatever amused you just on the promise of a job in your next picture. You could have your pick and almost none of the women were unattractive. Many were breathtaking.

Now Hitchcock, I ruminated, was not a handsome man. Oh, yes, he was impressive, but he wasn't anyone's idea of a romantic lead. I'd seen a lot of men like that. They know how they look. When they get into their fifties they begin to think what they've missed, and rush into the parlor of the first spider that seems willing. I still wasn't convinced that the great man hadn't been involved with Baby Lowen.

I must have been too wrapped up in my thoughts and didn't hear him until he was already in the house. I clicked out the desk lamp and slipped into the corridor. Luckily, he was looking into the sitting room. He spun on me with a face like an angry grizzly.

"You're home," I said. "Alma said I could wait."

"Not in my study," he said. "She wouldn't have done that."

"No," I said. "I was looking for a rest room."

"And you found it, I suppose?"

"Sure."

"I'm so glad."

I didn't know what to make of his tone of voice. There was a sarcastic tinge, though it wasn't harsh. I felt guilty from it, though. Like my father had caught me peeking up a girl's dress.

"I assume you have something to tell me," he said.

"I could wait until tomorrow if you're tired."

He pushed past me and led me into his study. He pulled the chain on his desk lamp and settled into his chair. The light from the lamp raked up his face, distorting it.

"You may begin."

"I'm sorry," I said. "I haven't got much."

"I'll be the judge of that," he said.

"I guess you will," I said. I summarized the day. So far I hadn't located any cops who had picked up Baby Lowen. "Are you sure," I asked, "that these were real cops, that they weren't just good costumes?"

He did not answer. After several seconds his stare made it impossible not to speak. "But," I said, "it's not at all clear that she was killed on Thursday." The only reason that they chose that time of death, I explained, was because it was as early as she could have been dumped without the bank employees seeing her, and also because of the coroner's assessment of the condition of the body.

"But that was just a guess. The day was warm, but who knows?"

"In your experience," asked Hitchcock, "is the coroner's judgment poor?"

"Well, I wouldn't say that exactly. I'm just saying there's no fact here to prove it either way."

"Go on."

"I did see a crime scene photo. She was missing her ear all right, but there were a lot of other parts missing, too." I then went on to describe my futile quest to get a photograph of Baby Lowen that clearly showed her right ear.

"Leonardo Ventuno," said Hitchcock slowly. He found the name funny.

"Have you heard of him?"

"Never. If he had photographed anyone who had auditioned for me, I would certainly have remembered the name. They usually stamp their names on the back. I have an interest in those who do portraits well."

"So he's a second rater."

"But it is essential we get a photograph of her."

I leaned forward, resting my elbows on my knees. "Why go through all this trouble to prove the ear's a match? Shouldn't we assume it's hers? The question is, why was it sent to you?"

"We can assume nothing, Mr. Slattery," he said sharply. "Perhaps you don't know who I am. You cannot conceive what strange artifacts come through the post. This is not the first body part, by any means. At least one was a great deal more intimate. The sender may well have wished to maintain the upper octave of his singing voice."

"Jesus," I said.

"No, I believe his name began with a B."

I shook off the image. "You're still dodging the question, Mr. Hitchcock. Did you know Baby Lowen? The answer stays in this room."

"I have told you I did not."

"Look," I said, "if you don't tell me the whole story, the whole truth, I can't help you. I'll go off on the wrong leads. I need to be able to trust you."

Hitchcock rocked forward in his chair, his nostrils hissing. "No, it is I who must trust you. If you wish to snoop in my study you could be man enough to admit it."

"Snoop?"

"The lamp," he said, settling back, "was still warm when I turned it on."

"Oh," I wittily rejoined. "Hey, I've been waiting here four hours, mister. I tried to go by your office, but they wouldn't let me on the lot. I'd have called, but you know they wouldn't have put me through. What the hell difference does it make if I see some of your notes and stuff? Have you got something to hide?"

I stood up and turned for the door. I figured I was fired.

His unique voice stopped me in my tracks. "Mr. Slattery," he said, "this is the number of my private secretary, Peggy Robertson. She can reach me at almost any time. There will likely not be a reason for your coming onto the lot, but if there is, she will arrange it."

"What makes you think I want to continue this job?"

"Please don't throw a tantrum. Actresses are frequently throwing them. Theirs are many times more impressive than you could ever manage. The result is always the same. They would not be working for me if they lacked the ability to do it. They would also not be working for me if they did not wish to." He inhaled. "I believe that their situation is quite similar to your own."

I took the notepaper on which he had written the number.

"Foolish people may believe actors endure working for me because of the money. I do not."

"I *do* expect to be paid."

"And you shall. Quite handsomely. But that isn't why you'll continue, first, to find the officers who arrested Miss Lowen and second, to get a photograph of her right ear."

"Okay," I said. "You're the boss."

"Good evening," he said. But the show wasn't over, not by a long shot.

CHAPTER SIX

M y phone rang about eight, a jackhammer in each ear.

"Who are you working for?"

"Huh?"

"The mayor's rattling my cage."

"Greene?"

"Who else? It has been suggested that I—off the record of course—cooperate with Mister Slattery. I assume that's you. I assume that means one of the studios is behind you. But let me tell you this, *Mister* Slattery, if the manure hits the fan I never heard of you and am shocked at the leaks in the department."

"I got it. So do I get to see what I want to see?"

Greene chuckled. "Who are you working for?"

I thought for a few seconds. I'd really ought to check with Hitchcock first. "The studio's all of a sudden interested in taking advantage of the news. Free publicity. So they're thinking about doing some true crime stories. Kind of B-level."

"They can't do the Baby Lowen story!"

"They'll leave out a lot. They might send me out to Kansas to look up her wholesome upbringing."

"She was from Iowa, bozo. Waterloo. Christina Marie Lowen. Family's in hogs."

"No wonder she wanted to get away."

"What do you mean?"

"You ever smelled a hog farm?" I snapped open the window shade to let the sunlight slap me awake. I needed to ask the right questions without giving anything in return. I asked if they'd tracked down any of her boyfriends, clients, sugar daddies.

"She met her Waterloo here," said Greene. He then went on to tell me she had been at several parties, mostly serving as a party favor. "But she had started to get pushy," said Greene, "so nobody wanted her around anymore."

"Blackmail?"

"Nothing anybody is singing about. Mostly it was just she wanted to collect on some of the promises."

"She started to demand some payback for her wear and tear."

"You got it. So they just stopped inviting her. Kept her out of the clubs. She made a scene at the Brown Derby trying to get to Errol Flynn. They bounced her."

"He knew her?"

"Only in the Biblical sense. Like he knew about half the floppers in town."

"Captain Blood waves a mighty sword," I said.

"It's got to have a dull blade by now."

"Who else?"

"If any of this gets in the paper—"

"It won't come from me."

He listed off ten or twelve other people whom she bragged about. Five of them were famous movie stars. Three of them said she had been at parties and other functions, but they hadn't touched her. Two admitted to sacking her, just once, of course. A few studio execs, casting directors, and agents took advantage of her giving nature as well. There were undoubtedly others. She had been a busy girl in her two years in Hollywood, but she hadn't held a regular job after the first six months when she'd tried the legendary Lana Turner route—working behind a drug store lunch counter.

"Is there anything in there about smoker flicks?"

The interest in Greene's voice immediately perked up. "You know something?"

I considered whether to bring up Leo Ventuno. "No, it's just the usual routine. Girl comes to town. Guy promises to get her on film. He just doesn't say what kind of film."

"We got nothing on that. What it was, she was showing up on people's doorsteps, at restaurants and bars, at the gates at MGM and Warner and Paramount claiming that this person or that said she was supposed to go in."

"It's ugly when the dream shakes hands with reality."

"It's a glittery town," said Greene matter-of-factly, "but a sad one."

I realized I was on thin ice with the next question. "If she was doing a lot of that, it makes sense a couple of cops would have picked her up for trespassing. Maybe she was looking for some star's house."

"Not on that Thursday. Not on that golf course."

"You checked?"

"None of the boys admit to leaving their cars in that neighborhood. Nothing much happens up there. Why would it?"

"Well, maybe it's a mistaken identity."

"Nobody picked up anybody up there," said Greene.

It struck me in a flash that maybe Hitchcock had made it up in order to get me to look into the murder for some other reason. But what was it?

"You finished?" Greene asked to my silence.

"No, I need a photo of her. She must have had a bunch of them somewhere to get into pictures."

"What we got wouldn't get her into anything but *Frankenstein.*"

"Thanks, cap. This might help. I appreciate it."

"The deal is you keep me posted," he growled. "You understand? Don't try to steal any of the credit."

"You're kidding me! I'm out of the collaring business."

"You can't collar, but you can steal credit. Don't try it or you'll be sorry. I'm not kidding about tipping me if you find out anything."

"Right," I said.

Actually, I never knew a single case in which a private eye made the cops look bad. We usually managed to handle that for ourselves. But everybody—Greene included—sees the movies and thinks the private detectives are always making the real detectives look like melon heads.

There wasn't any going back to sleep once the wheels started turning in my head. I decided to take another run by Ventuno's studio. I didn't think he was the kind of guy who would be hard at work before nine, but I thought maybe somebody lived upstairs.

When I got there, the place was as dead as ever. The trash was still in the front doorway. The back door had picked up a circus poster that had blown against it. I looked up and the window was open as it was before, the curtain hanging limp. If it ever rained, somebody would have a mess to mop up.

I glanced back at the alley. Nothing seemed to have changed except that trash day had been too long in coming. The smell was a casserole of dead skunk and my grand-mother's cabbage.

I crossed the street for coffee to clear the cobwebs from my brain and the smell from my nose. The counter girl in the drugstore still hadn't been discovered. I don't know why. She looked like she had started doing chest exercises at age four. The thin cotton blouse made it obvious. Deliberately obvi-ous.

"How's the coffee?" I asked.

"Hot and fresh," she winked. "Just like me."

"You've practiced that line, haven't you?" I smiled.

"Maybe I've been saving it for you." She said it breath-lessly, an over-the-top imitation of Marilyn Monroe. The phoniness of it didn't make it less inviting.

I sipped the coffee and felt my tongue go numb. "Yow!" I said. "You weren't kidding."

"Would I ever kid you?" she said, putting the pot back on the heater.

"How late do you work here?" I asked.

"Oooh," she said coolly, "you're a fast worker. I'm normally not available."

Normally? "That isn't what I meant," I said.

"Just my luck," she said.

"I was wondering if you'd ever seen anything going on across the street."

"You're the guy from yesterday."

I was a bit deflated. I had made such an impression. "Lights going on and off? Anything at all?"

"I think the upstairs light was on a couple of days ago."

"Days?"

"It was a morning, that's all I remember. Sunrise. The counter closes at two."

I squinted at the two upstairs windows. "I can't tell if it's on or off. You come to work at dawn? You wear six a.m. better than I do, than anybody I know does."

"Stars have to look their best at any time."

The coffee had dropped a few degrees. It was now merely painful. "How does that guy stay in business?"

"Beats me," said a voice. "He inherited it from his uncle, but he hasn't done much to keep it going." I rotated my stool and saw the pharmacist looking at me through his thick, tortoiseshell glasses. Mr. Peepers, I thought. "What is your interest in him?" he asked.

"I'm trying to get some pictures he took a few years back."

"You're not the only one asking about him," he said, shoving his glasses back up his nose and picking up a donut.

"There was a big guy with hands like this—" He gapped out at least six inches between the donut and his palm. "He said he needed to pick up some pictures."

Muscle, I thought. Leo owed the bosses money or, more likely, a few hundred feet of eight millimeter.

"I remember him," said the girl. "Sweated a lot. Needed a bath. I didn't like the way he looked at me."

"So you'd recognize him again?" I pulled Hitchcock's sketch out of my pocket. He had said one of the policemen was a big man. "Are either of these two the guy?"

They both looked closely at the sketches. "He was older," said the girl. "I think."

"Hey," said the pharmacist, "that woman there. She looks familiar."

"She favors Baby Lowen," I said cautiously.

"The actress who got murdered?" said the girl. "She's been in all the papers!"

And promoted to actress, I thought.

"That's where I know her," said the pharmacist. "That was a nasty business. Gad, what a world! She came in here a couple of weeks ago. She was asking for Mr. Ventuno. That was a couple of weeks, at least. I think. I'm not really sure."

"Did she say what she wanted with him?"

The pharmacist thought. "I don't know. I remember she was jittery, but exactly what she said—" He shrugged.

"Did she leave a number to call, anything like that?"

"No."

"Did you see her?" I asked the girl.

"She must have come in when the counter was closed."

The pharmacist squinted at the sketch again. "Baby

Lowen! Who'd have believed it? All she wanted was a break, you know. Like a lot of girls. Well, everybody knows who she is, was, now. Maybe she's finally happy with who she is."

"Seems like everyone's looking for Leo," I said. I swallowed the last of my coffee. There were grounds in it. She poured me another cup. A customer came in and the pharmacist went to the back. "Did Mr. Ventuno ever come in here?" I asked her.

Her eyes dodged a bit. She looked a little furtive. "Once or twice."

"He wanted to take your picture."

"He asked," she whispered, glancing back at the pharmacist. "He said I needed to circulate photos to show off my assets."

"He took photos of a lot of girls."

"And I know what kind, too." She blushed. A genuine blush. This surprised me. "Daddy told me he did girlie magazines. He tried to get daddy to carry them, but daddy's no pushover."

"Daddy?" I was beginning to see there might be a sixteen-year-old under that make-up. Holy mackerel, I thought. Even younger.

"Daddy was a Marine. Guadalcanal and Iwo Jima." She was looking back toward the pharmacist. "A Silver Star."

Mr. Peepers?

She leaned close and whispered. "Mom says he knows how to kill a man with his bare hands."

Mr. Peepers? Marine baloney. On the other hand . . .

"You—or your father—you give me a call if you see anything."

"I've got your number in the cash drawer. Come back any time. The coffee's always hot."

"And fresh," I said. I slapped a five on the counter and was gone.

CHAPTER
SEVEN

At first all I could think about was that maybe I had just missed being another one of those guys who says, "But she looked the legal age! I swear!" I'd arrested a few of them in my day.

But somehow the girl had given me an idea. It was so obvious I didn't know why I hadn't thought of it.

I spotted a phone booth and called Peggy Robertson, Hitchcock's assistant. I would later find out that she had worked for Hitchcock in London after the war, then joined him in America to work on the movie they were now making. All I knew at that point, however, was that she had a refined, efficient voice, and was obviously British.

"I am Chester Slattery," I said. "Mr. Hitchcock gave me this number."

"I know who you are, Mr. Slattery, but Mr. Hitchcock is about to go into conference with Henry Bumstead and the writers."

"Bumstead?" All I could think of was Dagwood and Blondie.

"He's the set designer. Can I have Mr. Hitchcock ring you?"

"Maybe you could help me." I explained what I wanted and the very efficient Mrs. Robertson told me who to see and that it would be arranged. Twenty minutes later I was greeting the guard who had kept me off the Paramount lot the day before. I followed his directions and was soon in the waiting room of the publicity offices. When I glanced down the corridor to my left, I saw Sig Fairfax going from one door to the opposite one across the hallway. I turned away.

"I'm Slattery," I said to the secretary, a beautiful brunette with green eyes.

"Oh, yes," she said. "Pleased to meet you." Her grating voice told me why she worked here rather than on a soundstage. She might be an extra, but she'd never get a line. She made Thelma Ritter sound like a songbird.

"You have the portfolios of people who apply for work here?"

"We store them for six months, then mail a postcard telling them to pick them up—unless they're hired."

"You don't keep them?" Damn, I thought.

"For six months. Two weeks after the post card."

It was worth a shot. "Can you see if you've got the portfolio of Christina Marie Lowen?"

The woman looked up.

"Yes," I said quietly, "Baby Lowen."

"Wow," she said. "And Alfred Hitchcock is interested in this?"

"He's doing me a favor," I said.

"It'll take a few minutes," she said, "but this I'll handle myself." She got an elderly woman in the nearest office to handle the phones, then disappeared into the back.

I scanned a *Variety* in the waiting room and noticed an article that said that shooting was beginning on Alfred Hitchcock's new thriller *From Among the Dead*. Kim Novak, it mentioned, had replaced Vera Miles, whom Hitchcock had originally wanted for the role. I didn't know whether it was true. Mokes like Sig Fairfax often planted phony stories to keep someone's name in print.

Once a story appeared that a B actor was on location trying out for the role of St. Peter. Actually, he was on location in a motel room dead from a hot shot of heroin, probably negotiating his permanent contract with St. Pete. Both stories ran concurrently on the same page of one paper. It was a bad moment for the *Hollywood Tattletale*.

I was beginning to think the girl had died among the file cabinets, but fortunately Sig Fairfax stayed in his office until she finally reappeared. I didn't want to draw his attention to me.

"She wasn't in the storage files," said the girl and I thought I'd have to try to get the portfolio from another studio or a casting director. "But she worked for us a couple of times."

"Really?"

She held out a folder. There were at least a dozen photographs in it. I pretended not to notice the one that revealed the beauty mark about three inches southwest of Baby Lowen's navel.

The girl pointed to a chart printed on the inside of the folder. "She was an extra on a couple of pictures." The girl almost pulled the folder away. "Wow," she said again, "that's ironic."

"What?"

"She was an extra on *The Wrong Man* last year. Did you see it? Henry Fonda. That's the only true crime story Hitchcock has filmed so far. I guess now he wants to film her story."

"She was an extra for Hitchcock?"

"That's what it says. And she was doing something with John Ferren a month ago."

"Who's John Ferren?"

"He's an artist. He does storyboards and incidental art. He's a pretty decent painter, I heard. Miss Lowen was to be paid through the art department of Hitchcock Productions, rather than Paramount."

I promised to return the folder within an hour. She made me sign for it, and I nearly broke the nib of the pen doing it. I was burning. Hitchcock had been lying to me. Why?

I got out of the publicity office as quickly as possible and walked into an office across the street to use their phone. Peggy Robertson barely got a word out of her before I jumped.

"I want to see the big man now! And I'm not waiting."

"Is this Mr. Slattery? Mr. Hitchcock cannot see you now."

"Well, you just tell him I'm on my way and he *will* see me."

"We're near the Bronson Gate. Come to suite 2-B in the middle of the administration building. By the time you arrive, perhaps something will be arranged. If your attitude improves."

"Lady, you ain't seen attitude yet!" I hung up, knowing full well that half a dozen security guards could greet me with a knuckle massage.

The secretary whose phone I had borrowed pretended not to be listening, but obviously was. Gossip hunger was second only to vanity in this burg. All those secrets that everybody knew were coin of the realm.

I burst into the office. It was large and plain with a temporary look. There was a foyer with two secretaries guarding two doors. One was lettered "Herbert Coleman, Associate Producer." The other was simply decorated with the simple line sketch of Hitchcock's profile. "Are you Robertson?"

The prim-looking woman I spoke to said nothing, but pointed to the second desk. Robertson's expressionless face was frozen in that hereditary British disdain for the colonials. She had frizzy raven hair and large, boxy glasses.

"And you must be Mr. Slattery?"

"Where is he?"

"Please sit," she said. "There. He will see you when he can."

"He'll see me now."

"Don't speak to me in that tone or you will be removed, Mr. Slattery. Sit!"

She was forceful enough in her grim way to make me hesitate. Before I could sort it out, a door opened. Two men came out carrying notebooks. The first one glanced at me, decided I wasn't important, and said "See ya, Peggy." I pushed past the second one and faced the almighty Hitchcock again.

"You lied to me," I said.

The two men looked in, Robertson moved between them. "Shall I get security?" she asked.

"You want us to handle it, Hitch?" said one of the men.

Hitchcock looked at me. "Writers have been known to kill with their scripts," he said.

"You'd better give me some answers and I mean quick—!"

Hitchcock cut me off me by raising his hand. "Peggy," he said, "an early lunch is in order. Take an hour."

"You sure everything's all right?" asked one of the writers.

"Except for Barbara's dialogue, Sam," grumbled Hitchcock.

"I'll fix it! I'll fix it!" he said in mock exasperation.

"A mere adjustment," said Hitchcock.

They closed the door and left. I expected some kind of outburst from the director. His neck was red from where it oozed out of his collar. The redness rose slowly to his thinning hair. I braced for an explosion, but he flustered me by saying calmly, "Barbara's dialogue makes little sense, given Midge's character."

"Who the hell is Barbara? Who is Midge?"

"She plays Midge."

I tried to get back on track. "Is she another woman you've seen out your back window?"

"I don't believe so. She's innocent but independent. I have her in mind for 'Lamb to the Slaughter.' Roald Dahl is a genius."

"Who—?" I didn't want to know. I must have gaped. I was in Wonderland.

"Have a seat, Mr. Slattery. You're carrying a folder."

I sat. I shoved it across the desk at him. "Explain this," I said.

"It appears to be a folder," he said. He stared at me for a moment, then flipped it open. He spread the pictures out on his desk. He lifted the nude of Baby Lowen. She was lying on satin in a Marilyn Monroe pose, her legs twisted to her right. Though her knees were together, just about everything was visible. Hitchcock scrutinized it and said, "And this appears to be a problem either for the wardrobe department or for hairdressing."

"No," I said, "explain the notation that says she worked for you on *The Wrong Man*. You knew her. You lied to me."

"I certainly did not, and I am offended you would say so."

"Be offended all you want. She was an extra on *The Wrong Man*."

He lifted a large magnifying glass, not a round one like you would see in a Sherlock Holmes movie, but a rectangular one with a tortoiseshell frame, about the proportions of a Vistavision screen. From where I sat, his eye looked the size of Moby Dick's. "So she was. It doesn't mean that I knew her."

"You know," I said, "you are not just some guy in the movie racket. You're Alfred Hitchcock. You can sketch two cops and a woman you saw for only a few seconds one evening. You see things like no one else does. You look at every frame of every movie you make. You're the ultimate craftsman. That's what you're famous for. Don't try to tell me you didn't know she was in there."

He looked at me coldly. "And you are forgetting who is your employer?"

"Employer? I haven't gotten a cent yet!"

"Mrs. Robertson will write you a check on my personal account."

I shook my head. "You're changing the subject again. What are you hiding about Baby Lowen?"

Hitchcock drummed his fingers. "Mr. Slattery, you are testing my patience. She could have been in the background of a shot on the street. She could have been in a shot taken by the second unit. She could have been in a scene that was dropped on the cutting room floor. I can arrange for a screening if you like. You will not find this woman in my film. You have come to the wrong conclusion."

"She was paid as an extra!"

"You may discuss it with Ward Monahan. He was in charge of herding the extras for the film."

"All right," I said. "All right. But what about the notation that she was hired to see John Ferren? That was supposed to be work on—whatever the new picture is. *From Among the Dead.*"

"It will be titled *Vertigo*. It will be a classic. Everything I direct, even my failures, are classics a year after they're released."

"How nice for you."

"John Ferren does various things involving art. He does storyboarding and paintings we might use on the set."

"So I understand."

"However, in this case, he was very busy. He asked if he might pass along some of his work to Walter Lamb. That is between you and me. Walter Lamb is an old acquaintance, but he suffers from periodic illnesses. He's not supposed to be hired, but he finds jobs on occasion to support his artistic pretensions. He's a painter."

"Of sets? Cars? What?"

"In this case of a portrait resembling Vera Miles. A woman becomes obsessed with a dead woman. She sits in front of her portrait at the museum. The detective, looking on, sees that they resemble one another, particularly in their hairdos."

"And what has Vera Miles to do with Baby Lowen?"

"Nothing, now. I was indisposed earlier this year, then there was trouble with the script, and then Vera decided to make a Tarzan, Jr. with Mr. Tarzan—her husband, Gordon Scott—so we signed Kim Novak. A portrait of Vera would no longer do. Walter instead was to paint one vaguely resembling Miss Novak. We hung it in the Palace of the Legion of Honor. They were very cooperative, though we wreaked havoc. The tourists were tripping over our cables.

"I don't know where the painting is now. Lamb will get it back eventually, I suppose."

"So Lamb was just the painter."

"Actually, John Ferren ended up painting the portrait after all. Lamb was unreliable per usual."

"But you didn't refer Baby Lowen to either one of them for any reason?"

He glared at me. I shouldn't have asked. It wasn't pleasant to be glared at by Hitchcock, and I've been glared at by some of the meanest bastards who ever committed a crime in Los Angeles.

"All right," I said. "I'll go talk to this Walter Lamb, and then to the extras guy."

"Ward Monaghan."

"Yeah." I stood. "But if I get the slightest whiff you're lying to me, I'm going to let the police know what I know."

"And what *do* you know, Mr. Slattery?"

It was an insult and he knew it. I didn't know much except what he'd told me, and that had no witnesses. It was all easy to deny. Who'd believe me, the defrocked detective?

He looked at the nude of baby Lowen again. "But we will know more very soon. Please lock the door."

I hesitated as he pulled a set of keys from his pocket and bent behind his desk. He fumbled with them and unlocked his lower desk drawer. I recognized the box as he set it on his desk. It was the one containing the ear. I threw the door latch.

"We are fortunate that her personal areas are not all that is uncovered in this photograph."

It was true. In the dozen or so clothed photographs, Baby Lowen's right ear was covered by her hair, or a hat, or she was facing the opposition direction and her right ear wasn't visible. In the nudie, however, her hair had fallen back. We could have used a larger image of her ear, but the print was very fine grained. Ventuno had used a large format negative.

He gingerly lowered the cold cream jar onto his blotter, then carefully unscrewed it. There was the faint smell of a vinegary preservative mixed with the residual smell from the Pond's. He rubbed his fingers together as if to get the touch of that jar out of them, then produced a large pair of tweezers from his top drawer. He lifted out the ear and placed it on a folded square of stationery.

He lifted his magnifying glass and examined the ear, then the photograph. The ear, then the photograph. If it weren't for the ear, it would have seemed funny to see him hunched over the nudie, his breathing audible, a dirty old man staring intently at his new treasure.

"She has this ridge here . . ." he said to himself. "The diamond earring in the photograph corresponds to the placement of the piercing."

He sat back and offered me the glass.

"Well, Mr. Slattery?"

I looked them over. Several times. At first I was sure, then I wasn't. I blinked to clear my eyes. Finally, I said, "I'd call it a match. I wouldn't swear to it, but they look the same to me."

"They are the same," said Hitchcock firmly.

"So it's hers."

"Did you ever really think it wasn't? Now we can be certain. This isn't a random prank like that finger last month or the chunk of liver last spring."

"Liver?"

"With a note signed by 'Saucy Jack the Lodger AKA the Ripper.'"

"Human?"

"Pork." He dropped the ear back into its liquid. "The question now becomes more interesting. Why was it posted to me?"

"Is there anything about the case that resembles any of your movies? Maybe the guy is imitating one of them."

"My films are about suspense, not carnage."

"Well, give it a thought," I said. "Don't you wish the guy had written down a return address?"

"What?" said Hitchcock. "And take all the amusement out of it?"

CHAPTER EIGHT

I got Ward Monahan's and Walter Lamb's phone numbers from Peggy Robertson, along with a most handsome check. A grand is pretty good for two days' work, but I knew there was a lot more to do. I stole a good headshot of Baby Lowen from the folder and tore up the nudie, dropping pieces of it in two trashcans on my way to return it to the publicity department. Freddy would have paid me three hundred dollars for that picture. Easy come, easy go.

Before I returned the folder, I took down whatever information I could get from it. Christina Marie Lowen had come to Hollywood from Waterloo, Iowa, when she was seventeen, according to the dates. She had looked a little older in her photographs. (You look at the neck and the hands for a pretty good guess.) But she might have shaved a couple of three years off, the way many another in this town lopped off a decade.

A lot of times people lied about their hometowns, too. It was good, generally, to come from the wholesome Midwest, bad to be from the Bronx or Hell's Kitchen. There were a lot of New York Jews passing for Kansas Presbyterians; Italians passing for full-blooded Apaches. A lot of peoples' backgrounds evaporated like politicians during a midnight raid on a cathouse.

Even though Baby Lowen seemed to have trouble hiding the dark circles under her eyes, her roundish face must have led to her nickname. Whether she brought the nickname with her or got it in Hollywood, I didn't know. She had changed addresses at least six times in the past year, notifying Paramount each time. Judging from the addresses, she moved upscale, then down, then further down, then far back up to some rather tony apartments. She moved from there to the kind of neighborhood where nobody ever saw nothin'—not the hookers, not the dopers, not the guy who shot his wife's boyfriend in broad daylight. Her roller coaster had a frightening drop. No wonder she was getting desperate in the last few weeks.

I tried my two leads in the movie business first. There was no answer at Lamb's. Maybe he was out playing Van Gogh in an olive grove. Monahan was "herding" a batch of extras in Monument Valley, Utah. He'd be back before the weekend, his landlord said.

I thought about driving out to Ventuno's place again. I had found a picture without him, but he probably knew more about her less savory activities than anyone else I could come up with. I decided I might be fooling myself, that I really just wanted to drool at the counter girl again.

Instead, I drove out to Baby Lowen's last address. There were about a dozen pink cottages, on a semicircle of macadam. I figured the place to be an old motor hotel that had gotten swallowed by the growing city. All of the tiny cottages were peeling. Half were beginning to list.

The door was open where Baby Lowen had lived, half off its hinges. There was no mattress on the bedsprings and the bathroom mirror was smashed.

"Are you with the police?" asked a gravelly voice. A skinny woman in a faded muumuu stood just outside the door.

"No, I'm a private cop. This is where Baby Lowen lived?"

"You're not with no paper? I'll tell you all you want to know for fifty bucks. I know all about her."

"I'm not with a paper. I'm a private eye. She owed my client some money."

The woman cackled. "Well, your client's out of luck. I was about to kick the slut out. She was behind a week."

"You rent by the week?"

"By the hour, if I have to. I was hoping you was the police, so's I could rent that one out again. I went over to get myself a pint the other night and somebody busted in. They throwed her clothes all over."

"Did they take anything?"

"Nothing to take but her clothes. The police took anything else."

"What did they take? The police."

"Her jewelry case."

"She had jewelry?"

"No. But they took her case. A cheap thing."

"Any idea why they took it?"

"No. She kept some phone numbers in it. In match books. I seen her put one there once."

I reached in my pocket and pulled out a ten. I snapped it so the woman could salivate. "I can't pay you much, but anything you could tell me about her might be a help."

"It's gotta be worth two of those."

"How would I know that?"

"Twenny," she said, but she didn't look steady.

"Ten now and ten if it's worth it."

She reached out to snatch the ten from my hand. She missed. I held it out.

"Ten now and ten if it's worth it."

"Come on out of the sun," said the woman. We sat in what passed for her kitchen. When she moved her bourbon bottle off the counter, two bugs ran in opposite directions.

She rambled for about an hour. She and Baby had shared a few long evenings getting potted and reviling every man who ever lived, beginning with Adam in the Garden of Eden and moving on to Iowa pig farmers to actors who ride and shoot blanks. "Nothing personal," she said, "but she and me been done wrong a lotta times, if you know what I mean."

What does a man say to this? I said, "Yes, ma'am."

Baby had gotten a lot of promises from all sorts of Hollywood banana slugs and very rarely collected on them. She tossed the names of actors, directors, and producers around as if they were all friends of hers. Billy Wilder had noticed her at a party. Hal Wallis had told her to drop by his office. Jeff

Chandler advised her that a lot of good work was going on in Italy and that was the place to become a star. Edith Head wanted to design a dress for her, but Baby wondered if she was "funny." And so on. And so on.

"Did you believe any of this?" I asked.

She shrugged. "You can't kid a kidder. A few things at first, she still seemed wet behind the ears, but they kept coming, don't you know. So she'd been at a couple of parties. So what? Hollywood is a party and most of the people there are extras. The potted plants are more important than the potted guests, don't you know. She still had her looks. If you got the looks you can go just for the canapés, eh?"

"Did you believe she really knew any of these people?"

"She had an autograph book, and there were a lot of names in there. Errol Flynn wrote something sweet, but I can't remember what it said."

The woman cackled. A blast of bourbon breath scorched my face. "She said he wasn't as good as he was supposed to be."

"What happened to the autograph book?"

"I told her she could sell it to some collector, maybe. Or pawn it."

"To pay your rent."

"Hey, sentiment's for suckers, handsome. I gotta live, too."

In a manner of speaking, I thought. "Was anything going on with Baby in the last few weeks?"

She thought. It was an effort.

"I didn't see her much just before she was killed." Something popped in her pickled brain. "A man came by."

"A man?"

"Elvis hair. A lotta dabs'll do ya. He knocked on my door, asked if I was the landlady."

"Yeah?"

"Said to tell her to call him. Had a job for her. Somebody had seen her pictures."

"Her pictures?"

"Said something about she looked like Kim Novak. Hell, I seen her in *The Eddy Duchin Story,* and I didn't think Baby was much like her."

"Kim Novak?"

"Yeah."

"What do you think he meant?"

"Hell, mister, I don't know. Maybe he wanted to con some out-of-towner."

Oh, yes, I thought, that old dodge. Offer the businessman from Pittsburgh a chance to sleep with a real movie star, a movie star who gets a kick out of banging strangers, a movie star who's a nympho. But she likes to get paid, she does. How much would you pay to do Marilyn Monroe, Jayne Mansfield, Rita Hayworth, Betty Grable, Esther Williams, you name her. When I was a rookie cop a girl died from a beating because the patsy figured out she wasn't Joan Crawford. She didn't even resemble Joan Crawford. It still took the patsy an hour to figure it out. By then she was down to her garters.

"Do you remember the name of the guy who came around?"

"He left his card."

"Well?"

"Well, I threw it out. Do I look like Western Union?"

"No," I said, "you sure don't."

"You don't remember the name?"

"Volare? Leonardo Da Vinci? Something wop."

"Ventuno," I said.

"Who?" she said. Her eyelids and her head were sinking like a sun that's been up for a week. I stood to leave and dropped another ten on her table.

"Hey," she said, "don't go. Tell me about yourself. Have another drink."

"My wife wouldn't approve," I said.

"So what's a wife got to do with it?" she cackled.

Once more I found myself fighting traffic to Ventuno's picture parlor. Once again there was no answer, and no sign anyone had been there. The upstairs window in the back was still open. The lunch counter girl wasn't in, but her father (Mr. Peepers, hero of Iwo Jima) hadn't noticed anything.

I drove home and took a nap. Finding Leo Ventuno was going to take a while, and trolling among the bottom feeders always takes a lot of energy.

CHAPTER NINE

I got up about seven p.m., showered and shaved, then grabbed a bite at a chophouse. I thought about briefing Hitchcock on what I'd found out, but when I saw the woman in the phone booth bawling, I decided to wait for a drier handset. Mentally, I made a list of the clubs most likely to be entertaining Ventuno's gangster friends.

Pete Cohn was the most likely person to know where Ventuno was. Cohn had changed his name from Cohen and allowed people to believe he was related to Harry Cohn, the mogul at Columbia. When I was on the force, we knew how Pete recruited most of his girls of many talents. There was always a surplus of down-on-their-luck girls, runaways who'd been told, or dreamed, they were beautiful enough to be movie stars. His men got a bounty for picking them up, taking them to what was supposed to be a place to meet celebrities, and then convincing them that the stage show at Cohn's kootchie bar, The Knight Klub, was the cat's pajamas for sophisticates who worked in the movie biz.

Hey, well, chickie, if you want to make it in this town you've got to make it in this town. Soon the girls were kootchie dancers, call girls, and actresses—maybe I should say "performers"—in the latest Pete Cohn smoker flick.

The porno was filmed in LA. The negatives were copied onto eight-millimeter stock in Mexico, and the copies shipped somehow into the ports of New Orleans and New York. An occasional batch was intercepted, usually by mistake, but no one had ever been able to pin charges on Cohn. A few low-levels had been fined. The Mexican police never found anything—so they said—in the suspected printing plants. How Cohn got his dirty pictures all over the states from the ports remained a mystery.

The postal inspectors tried for years to nail him for anything: one frame of dirty film, a solicitation, anything. They came to the conclusion he didn't use the mails. It was convenient not to have to look for his stuff anymore.

I arrived at The Knight Klub about nine. It wasn't easy to park. There were lots of cars in the parking lot, Cadillacs and Lincolns, some big Buicks, a cream-colored Olds convertible, and even a pair of Rolls Royces. Despite the crowd, the low-slung building was eerily silent. It was soundproofed.

I remembered a story that in 1954 there had been a major shoot-out in there over the horse trade. Some thugs made the world a better place by ventilating six other thugs. Nobody in the area heard a thing.

Based on the word of a snitch, cops went over the place with metal detectors. They found one flattened Tommy gun bullet in a newly plastered wall. "Now how did *that* get in there?" asked Pete's night manager.

A very large man in a dapper suit leaned against a gold Lincoln reading a newspaper. His head and face turned from blue to red to blue as the neon sign blinked. I recognized him as Arnie, Cohn's chief bodyguard and enforcer.

"So," I called out, "Pete's in tonight, is he?"

He looked at me suspiciously. "Maybe he is and maybe he ain't. Who're you?"

"I wanted to talk to him about the movie trade. It'd be great if Leo Ventuno's here, too."

"Ventuno? You know Ventuno?"

"He's an acquaintance. I wanted to talk to them both about the movie trade."

"Beat it. Mr. Cohn ain't in the movie business."

No, I thought, I wouldn't call them movies, either. "You know what I mean. I thought maybe you could get me inside."

"If you ain't a member, Pete don't want to talk to you. Beat it."

I shrugged, then reached into my jacket with my right hand. "Well, could you give him my card?"

The movement of my hand into my chest pocket made Arnie drop one end of the paper and go for the artillery in his armpit. Before the gun came out, I stepped closer, holding out a laundry ticket.

"Shove your card," he snarled.

When he glanced down at the comics section on the

ground, I raised my Smith and Wesson out of my left pocket.

He dropped the rest of the paper and thought about going for his shoulder holster.

"Don't," I said. "Nobody's getting hurt. Just get me in to talk to Mr. Cohn. I've got business."

"You'll get hurt for getting the drop on me, creep."

"Just get me in, Arnie. I'll give you the gun when I see Cohn."

I got behind him and, as we moved toward the entrance, told him to lower his hands. He pushed the button under the sign, "MEMBERS ONLY." A speakeasy slit in the door opened.

"It's me," said the thug. "Let me in."

Latches clacked in succession. A tidal wave of music poured out. I got up close behind him and was ready to follow when he dove forward. Hands shot out of the dark inside. Before I could react, something came down hard on my forearm and my gun fell away. I couldn't see who had got me. There was a flash of a man with a big chin who just missed me with a sap. Hands yanked me forward by the lapels, and my face cracked against the big man's shoes. I tried to roll over before the sap found my skull, but they clamped down on my arms and legs, pinning me to the floor like an insect specimen. Slowly, then, they peeled back my arms and I felt handcuffs squeezed hard around my wrists. I thought of my ankle piece and how many miles away it was down my leg. I also thought how being a cop got you a little deference, or at least someone watching your back.

Arnie stood. He pressed one of his size fifteen wingtips on the back of my neck and put his weight on it. He bellowed something I couldn't hear. I thought he was going to break my neck. I tried to shout but he was choking off my wind.

He went down on one knee and shouted in my ear. "Who are you, you son-of-a-bitch?"

"I'm a cop. I need to talk to Mr. Cohn."

He grabbed the back of my head and banged it once against the floor. Blood filled my nostrils.

They jerked me to my feet. I was in a small foyer with a coat checkroom to the side. I could see through the glass panels in the swinging doors. The image froze in my brain like a snapshot.

There was a woman on stage in a shaft of purple light. She was doing unnatural things with a crookneck squash. The drowsy man at the front table was nodding off like it was the fiftieth act of *The Ring of the Nibelungs*. The woman beside him was more interested. She seemed to think it was a comedy.

They jerked me past a girl cowering in the coat checkroom and through a door. They dragged me down a corridor with silly pink wall lights and through another door. I was in an office. It was decorated like it belonged to Fu Manchu.

"The blood's getting on the rug," said the big man to the bouncer with the big chin. "Get a rag or something! And send Peewee out to the car. Tell him to check it good."

He looked at me. His scarlet face looked sunburned from the effort. The gray bristles in his crew cut sparkled with beads of sweat.

"Stop bleeding!" he shouted at me.

"I just wanted to talk to Mr. Cohn," I sniffed.

He flipped open my wallet, then looked at me again. "The guy's carrying a check signed by Alfred Hitchcock," he said.

One of the bouncers stared at it. "Hey, whattaya know!"

"How do you know Alfred Hitchcock?"

"None of your business," I said.

He raised back his hand. I tried to remember a quick prayer, any prayer. But he didn't hit me.

"Get Mr. Cohn," he said.

The lighting was dim. The Chinese paper shades gave everything a pink tinge. The office was all black lacquer, tassels, and writhing dragons. There was a large sofa. I figured it got a regular workout from the stage performers.

Cohn came into the office after a few minutes. He was a small man with pudgy hands and a nose somebody had flattened for him when he was an aspiring subhuman in a tenement.

"You don't look so good," he said to me.

"I don't feel so good," I said.

He pinched the bridge of my nose and jerked it from side to side.

"Hey," I said, trying to stand up. Cohn shoved me back onto the chair.

"It's all blood. It isn't even broken." He sat on the edge of his desk. "Yet."

"I interrupted your show."

"Seen it. So has anybody who's been to Tijuana. Sort of. You might say I adapted it." He lit a cigarette and offered it to me. I shook my head.

"Arnie—" he tossed his head toward the big bodyguard "—tells me you're looking for Leo."

"Is he out there?"

"Mr. Cohn will ask the questions here," said Arnie.

"Yeah, I'm looking for Leo."

"Why?" asked Cohn.

"He owe you, too?" asked the bodyguard.

"Arnie . . ." warned Cohn. "Well?"

"I'm trying to find out what he knows about Baby Lowen."

"Baby—? Isn't that the one that got carved?"

"Yeah," I said. "Did you do it?"

Cohn grinned. "I carve turkeys, not girls. A girl's no good carved. She just lies there. Can't use the ones that just lie there."

"Ventuno took her pictures. Some of them were nudies. Maybe he made some smokers with her?"

"I imagine that footage like that would sell pretty good now that she's a celebrity. I mean if somebody was in that business, there's a profit window there. In a year, who cares about the slut?"

"So you knew her?"

"Who told you that?"

"Leo knew her. It makes sense you did."

"It makes nothing, Slattery. Don't come around here impersonating a cop with me. You're the bozo that got kicked off the force." He turned to Arnie. "This is the guy that took out Smoky Tex Grady. The cowboy star."

"I don't like westerns," said Arnie.

"That's un-American. I ought to report you. You think I ought to report him?"

"Smoky Tex gotta be a pansy, this guy could take him."

"He's a member," said Cohn. "Uses the name Theodore West."

"Him?"

"Yeah, him. You went to a few good American movies you'd have recognized him right off."

"Maybe we should invite him back to get even," said Arnie.

"Maybe," said Cohn.

"Look, Mr. Cohn," I said, "punching Tex wasn't the stupidest thing I ever done, but maybe coming in here was. I thought Leo was in here. I didn't know you were looking for him, too. You sent Arnie out to look for him, didn't you? At the drugstore across the street he asked about Leo."

"I don't know what you're talking about," said Arnie.

"It means nothing to me," I sniffed. "I'm just trying to find out what happened to Baby Lowen. I know Leo took her pictures. I know he was looking for her. I figure he might have got her into a smoker. Or maybe he was pimping her."

Cohn suddenly turned red. "Or maybe she worked here? Is that what you're getting at?"

"Did she?"

"You suggest that to anybody, Slattery, you'll be part of a bridge."

I thought of the six mobsters who disappeared one night several years ago. I was now certain they were somewhere in a bridge. I'd probably driven over them. I almost swallowed my Adam's apple. Was Ventuno?

I again thought how far away that gun on my ankle seemed.

Cohn paced for a minute and stubbed out his cigarette. "What's Hitchcock got to do with you?"

"He had a break-in, nothing was stolen but—"

"Arnie, make this guy tell the truth."

Arnie moved toward me.

"Wait," I said, talking fast. "It's like this. The movie he made last year, *The Wrong Man,* it's a true story. It's the only true story he's done. He liked doing it. He's thinking about another one."

Arnie glanced at Cohn, who was suddenly interested. "No kidding?" Cohn asked.

"He thought I was good to look into a few things with the police, since I know the guys. He's trying to find out if there's a movie in, well—"

"Baby Lowen. It's like the Black Dahlia. I said it right off. Didn't I, Arnie?"

Arnie nodded.

"The Black Dahlia was good for a couple of movies, I think. Of course they had to change the details."

"That's not my end of it," I said. "He has writers for that."

Cohn had the beatified gleam of someone who has now learned one of Hollywood's secrets. He thought for a moment. "Okay, look, you find Ventuno and you get what you want out of him. But if you find him, you let me know."

"What's he into you for?"

"It's personal. Just a little something I need to discuss with him. We've been looking for him for a good week. Nobody's seen him."

"You think he killed the girl and took a powder?"

"Leo? He was a sweet-talker. He never had to slap any girl. It was a gift. If he got her number he could talk her into anything, sell iceboxes to Eskimo babes."

"Maybe Baby wasn't buying."

Cohn stared at me for a second. How could a guy that looked so ordinary have such power? The evil that flickered in his eyes had returned.

"You ever try to get in here with a gun again, remember what I said, you'll be holding up a highway."

"No thanks," I said.

"And I did you a favor."

"A favor."

"I didn't bring Smoky Tex back here to geld you."

"You're a true friend," I said.

"Find Leo for me," he said. He straightened his bow tie, then swept the hair at his temples to make sure it was still in place, and went back to his club.

CHAPTER
TEN

After Arnie dumped me on the pavement next to my car, he held me down with his big foot in the middle of my back while he unlocked the handcuffs.

"I'll get you for this," I hissed through my teeth.

"You and what army?" he laughed. He emptied my Smith and Wesson, dropping the cartridges into his pocket, then flung the gun into the back seat of my car.

As he walked away, I bent and touched the ankle piece they hadn't noticed. Arnie could take all eight of its little bullets and still strangle me. I decided to let it ride and took some comfort in the thought that maybe one day they'd forget to completely search a guy who was preparing Pete Cohn to hold up a bridge.

I looked at myself in the rear view mirror. Like the

proverbial newspaper, I was black and blue and red all over. I hadn't looked so bad since I got a tree limb in the face parachuting into St. Mere Église in 1944. Thirteen years ago, I thought, I was twenty-three and healed about thirteen times faster. Maybe a hundred times faster.

There were still at least six bars or clubs where Ventuno might be hanging out, but I now looked like a plate of roasted peppers. Besides, if Ventuno was making the rounds, Pete Cohn would know it. He, or his buddies higher in the mobster pecking order, would have eyes and ears in every bar. Doing a favor for the Cohns of this world was generally a smart thing in the booze trade. And Ventuno would know it.

What had he done to anger Pete Cohn? It could have been a thousand things. Not paying the vig. Not delivering a smoker print on time. Putting Cohn in some kind of jeopardy by talking to the feds. Or telling one of the bosses something that Cohn didn't want them to know.

Maybe Ventuno knew something about Cohn and Baby Lowen. Cohn had influence. Baby Lowen wanted help. Cohn was always very helpful to lost girls. Cohn was exactly the kind of man she'd flop for, maybe several times, maybe with several "friends" of Cohn's. Maybe Cohn killed her?

In some kind of rage he might. But he didn't get to be in charge by overreacting. He'd do a slow burn, make sure he could get away with it, and use Big Arnie and the minions for his dirty work. That was part of being a boss: "The guy did what? I don't know nothing about that, officer." If Baby gave him some trouble, he'd just tell Big Arnie to take out the garbage, and that would be all anybody ever heard of Baby again.

That could have happened.

On the other hand, my instinct told me it was more likely Ventuno killed her and was now on the run. Where would a guy like that go? He didn't seem the kind of guy for hiding out in the Sierra Nevadas with the chipmunks and coyotes. Las Vegas, maybe? Cohn would know, then. Maybe Cohn did know and was just pulling me around by my eggplant of a nose.

I remembered a truck stop near the highway. Open all night, it had a few shirts for sale. I pulled in and bought the least obnoxious one that fit me. There was a cactus embroidered on the pocket flap. A clerk that looked like she had come to California with Ma Joad said, "Whee-oh! That's a nasty double shiner there!"

"Accident," I said.

When I washed up in the restroom, a raccoon who'd gone a few rounds with Jersey Joe Walcott stared back at me from the mirror.

I got some change and went to the phone booths. A couple of truckers were calling home, but one got off soon. I dialed Hitchcock's home number.

"I'll see if he's in," said the maid, then the world-famous voice said, "Good evening."

I summarized my evening.

"You may include whatever medical expenses you incur," he said, "but try to avoid such situations in the future. Death is a lengthy—and I'm sure, boring—experience."

"I'll avoid my own funeral at all costs."

Hitchcock hmmed. "I am quite tired, but it would seem to me that the whereabouts of Mr. Ventuno might not be relevant at all."

"A lot of people are looking for him."

"But for what reason?"

"You have a point. But he might be able to tell us something useful about Baby Lowen."

"Indeed."

I thought of something from earlier. "Tell me, do you think Baby Lowen resembles Kim Novak?"

"Only in a superficial way. Her frame is quite similar. Her face is less womanly, more childish. Her superstructures are much less impressive than Miss Novak's are. The photographs of Miss Lowen are more Marilyn Monroe than Miss Novak."

"She wasn't being considered as what's it called? Somebody who takes the place of an actress when she's got to powder her nose, when the back of her head's the only thing in the shot."

"Miss Novak has a stand-in. Miss Lowen was never considered by me."

I sniffed, trying to get a normal flow of air through my nose. Enough came through to tell me the phone booth had been cleaned with Lysol. "There's something sad and attractive about Baby Lowen. You can see that in the photos, but I don't know why Ventuno thought she could be a match for Kim Novak. Maybe he was just lying to her, like everyone else."

"Sad and attractive? Pity, Mr. Slattery?"

"Not really. She made her bed. But I can feel sorry for her."

He hmmphed. "If you are falling in love with a dead woman, be certain you tell me in detail all about it."

"'Laura is a mist in the empty night . . .'"

Hitchcock hmmphed again. I wasn't clear whether he disapproved of Otto Preminger's movie *Laura,* the theme song, or the fact I had made a joke. It was the only movie I could think of in which a detective falls for a dead woman.

"By the way," he told me, "the lie about my being interested in filming the Baby Lowen story has become quite useful. Quite."

"Grist for their mills," was all I could think to say.

He hmmphed again, then said "Good evening." I was left with the feeling the conversation should have been longer.

I sat in the booth a second trying to decide what to do next. Searching the bars seemed pointless. It was pretty late to call Lamb. I decided to do the obvious thing, the thing I had been avoiding.

Parking a block away from Ventuno's studio, I took my tire iron and flashlight from the trunk and slipped up the alley. A dog threw himself against one of the fences in a fit of barking, but I moved along quickly and no one came out of the house. I could see the second floor window was still open. The curtains stirred on a light breeze.

I was about to lift the gate latch when I noticed Ventuno's trashcans in the alley. I checked both ways, saw no one, and as quietly as possible lifted the lids. Both were empty. No one had taken out the trash for a while.

The latch took some rattling to open. I moved across the back yard to the heavy door. I knew from police work that people often install a thick, heavy door, but don't install a lock to match. I wedged the sharp end of the tire iron between the door and frame. The wood gave way, but it did not open, even when I threw a shoulder into it hard enough to make my ears ring. I flicked on my flashlight and found a stone about the size of a cinnamon roll, which I shoved against the doorframe as a fulcrum. I pressed the tire iron until my palms went numb. The wood cracked. The bolts holding the inside latch gave way.

I took a quick look to see whether anyone had noticed. A plane hummed high overhead. I closed the door and turned on my flashlight. I bumped my ankle piece with my heel for assurance.

There were stairs to my left going down to a door with a warning light above it. The darkrooms, I presumed. There were also stairs above, going up towards the rear. The back door was the access to the rooms upstairs. To my right was a set of fuse boxes, far more than an ordinary building would need. Most of the feeds went down, but one went up. A lot of electricity was going into the cellar, with only a routine power line to the rooms.

In front of me was another locked door. I rapped on it, heard nothing. It had a simple skeleton key lock. It would have been easy to kick in, but every noise seemed ten times louder than it should. I used the tire iron to force it. The streetlight oozed through the dirty front windows.

As my eyes adjusted, I could see I was behind a counter. To my right was a Speed Graflex on a tripod and several lights arranged in a semicircle around a wingback chair and a rack of backdrops. In front of the counter was a sitting area with two old-fashioned sofas, ashtray stands at each arm, and a coffee table with magazines I couldn't make out in the dim light. It looked like Ventuno hadn't changed anything since he'd inherited the place. He didn't seem like a candidate for sentimental guy of the year.

When I backed in to the Graflex and nearly knocked it over, I felt a thick layer of dust on it. Nobody had been in the front for years. It certainly hadn't been used for sittings.

I slowly climbed the stairs to the second floor. The door at the top stood half open. I pushed it. The curtains on the window opposite leapt up at me like a specter. I nearly fell back into the dark of the stairwell. My heart pounded and I could feel the pulse in my face.

Although it had been dark for hours, the heat of the day still radiated down from the ceiling. I moved away from the cool of the window, and lowered the flashlight.

The three rooms beyond the landing constituted the ultimate bachelor pad. A well-stocked bar, an expensive hi-fi, Mantovani and Sinatra records, a thick carpet, and a low-slung make-out sofa filled the main room. There was a bathroom with a leopard pattern shower curtain and matching fuzzy mats and toilet cover.

The height of lousy fashion was the bedroom. It had a big, heart-shaped bed that must have been shipped from a Las Vegas honeymoon hotel. Mirrors on the ceiling. Convenient stereo and light switches beside the headboard. Heart-shaped ashtrays on the end table. In the drawer, the wrapper from a French tickler and an empty pack of matches:

Meet the Elite
at
THE KNIGHT KLUB
Members Only

The walls were draped in pink satin. Opposite the bed, I yanked them back, expecting to find a camera. There was nothing but water stains in the old plaster. There wasn't even a wall plug except behind the headboard. If they filmed in there, they'd have to run heavy extension cords from other rooms. This really was Ventuno's personal playroom, I thought, and remembered all the electrical lines going downstairs.

I thought I heard a creak. I listened at the top of the stairs, but everything was silent. I decided it was the old building stretching its joints.

Slowly climbing down the stairs, I saw that the back door had opened. Wind? I hadn't noticed the curtains move upstairs. The door creaked again when I shut it. I checked outside, heard the dog barking, and was about to prop something against the door when I froze.

The darkroom door in the cellar was open. My empty Smith and Wesson was still in my car. The popgun on my ankle piece was better for swatting flies, but it would have to do. Maybe Leo had come home. Maybe he was dialing the police. Maybe. Maybe. Maybe.

I took it one step at a time, stopping halfway when a light flicked on, slicing the stairway in half. There was rustling. Drawers opening and closing. Papers and tinny things hitting the floor. I eased down the dark side of the staircase, took a breath, and dared a quick look.

A big man in an expensive dark suit was searching a long row of file cabinets. His back was to me. I didn't get a good look at him. Film canisters lay on the floor among scattered negatives. I gripped my flashlight firmly and thought about going back upstairs for my tire iron or better artillery.

There was a laugh then, followed by a rumbling noise, loud thumping, then a crack as a door gave way.

I glanced again. A section of the file cabinets sat at an odd angle. It had been pulled forward away from a door disguised with phony brick. The man had moved into the next room, muttering to himself. I heard the clink of an overhead light chain.

The secret studio, I thought. Porn central station.

I bent low and crept into the darkroom. Two enlargers and a set of developing trays sat on the counter opposite. Beneath the counter were rows of dark-brown chemical bottles on wooden shelves.

And one odd thing rested on top of a yellow box labeled "Kodak Fixer."

A Pond's Cold Cream jar.

The same large economy size as the one mailed to Hitchcock.

In my moment of surprise, the big man charged back through the door on his way out. He skidded to a stop on the scattered negatives when he saw me and nearly fell. It was Pete Cohn's thug Arnie. "Slattery!" he said. His hat caught the overhead light and it began to swing.

I held out my popgun and said, "I'll shoot," just in time to have the developing clock flung at me. I ducked but it caught me on the shoulder. My feet went out from under me as I fired, puncturing the top of the enlarger.

Arnie was going for his gun.

Hitting the floor hard on my back, I kicked at Ernie's legs and caught a shin. He staggered, grabbed the counter, and I fired again. Arnie was no fly. If I hit him, it made no difference. He growled and pushed a file cabinet at me. It broke the heel off my shoe as I skittered towards the door, but it blocked his way for just a moment. He climbed over it and was introduced to my flashlight. Once.

Twice.

Three times.

He expelled a stream of air like a giant bull having a nightmare and collapsed on top of the cabinet. My flashlight was bent like a pileup of Ramblers. My arm ached and I knew I had hit him hard enough to kill him. I put my popgun to his temple and felt under his ear. There was a pulse in his neck.

I patted him down, expecting to find whatever he'd taken from the hidden room. There was nothing unusual, the .45 Army Colt in his armpit and the handcuffs he had used on me. The cuff barely fit around his wrist. I hooked the other end to the iron water pipe under the counter.

The Pond's jar had fallen back on the shelf during the struggle. I reached back into the spider webs and pulled it out. Liquid moved in it. As I set it on the counter, Arnie moaned, but did not wake up.

Gingerly, I unscrewed the lid. Inside was a clear liquid similar to that in Hitchcock's jar. There was also a chunk of something.

Meat. The shaking in my hands passed to the jar. The chunk rotated. It was the tip of a nose.

I gripped the edge of the sink, but managed to keep from vomiting. I had seen worse as a cop. Car accidents. The derailment in 1953. But this was more personal, somehow. I had seen Baby Lowen's glamour photos. I had seen her posed in the nude. When you wear a badge, you wear it over the heart. Maybe when you lose your badge, you lose your shield.

I recovered enough to look at the inside of the Pond's lid. "ALL OF YOUR'S" was scratched into the metal. How many of these had Ventuno mailed out? Who else was on his mailing list?

I checked on Sleeping Beauty, then went through the phony door. It was a closet-sized anteroom with a jacket hanging on a wall peg. At the back was another door, heavy and soundproof. When I yanked the handle, a sweetish foul odor washed over me, an odor I recognized. I knew what was in there. I just didn't know who.

CHAPTER
ELEVEN

I threw a tray of water in Arnie's face and slapped him half a dozen times. His jaw rolled and he came around, my ankle piece crossing his eyes. For the first time, I noticed that one of my shots had nicked him under his holster.

"Did you do that?" I said.

He shook his head, his eyes jiggling like Mamie Van Doren's bumpers. He squinted at my bruised and swollen face as if I was materializing in front of him but the rabbit ears needed adjusting. "I didn't do nothing," he said. "I want my lawyer."

"In there. You knew he was here."

"I just found him."

"You're lying."

"No." His eyelids flapped. I was losing him.

I rapped his wound with my fist. "You knew where the studio was."

"I never been here."

"Why don't I believe you, Arnie? A birdie told me you asked across the street about Leo. And you went straight down here. You didn't search."

"Cohn told me. The basement."

"He told you to clean up the mess."

"No."

"Cohn knew he was dead down here."

"No."

"Who do you think the police will believe? You? Me?"

"Mr. Cohn said there might be a smoker of Baby Lowen."

"You were looking for film?"

"He thought it might be valuable."

I remembered Cohn's remark that a movie of the murdered girl would be worth a lot. He must have decided to send Arnie after it. It made sense, too much sense. Arnie had been searching for something. But that didn't mean that Arnie hadn't killed Ventuno a few days ago.

"Ventuno owed Mr. Cohn three thousand. He thought the film might be worth a couple."

"What did he owe him for?"

"I dunno."

I whacked the wound again. "Try again."

"I don't know, damn it. You'll make it bleed."

He caught his breath. I raised my fist again.

"He backs the supplies. The film stock. Ventuno's got to bribe somebody to develop it, see. He picked up the money

Friday at lunch, then he skipped."

"Why did Ventuno kill Baby Lowen?"

"I dunno. How would I know? I didn't know he did. There was no reason to kill her. She wasn't used up yet."

I almost shot him for saying that. I cracked his forehead with the butt of the gun.

I was too rattled to think. What was I missing? In the porno studio, Leo Ventuno had two sixteen-millimeter cameras, an assortment of lights, and various props. A big bed, of course. A cat o' nine tails. Candles. Shackles with heavy chains. The oddest thing was a stuffed eagle with spread wings. It was hard to see it as a sex prop.

One set of the shackles had been used to hold Leonardo Ventuno in the claw-legged bathtub. The chain ran underneath the tub from one wrist to the other. The chain had scraped the tub violently as the Photographer of the Stars struggled.

His throat had been slit from ear to ear, but that had been an act of mercy. His head lolled over the back rim of the tub as if he were asleep.

The killer had pulled Ventuno's guts out of his belly. Judging from the chain marks, while he was alive.

I thought I ought to go back in there. Something that would help sort all this out might be in plain view. I stepped into the anteroom and hesitated. The smell was too much for me. With other cops there it would have been a question of manhood. Who needs this? I thought. Instead, I reached into the pocket of the motorcycle jacket hanging on the peg.

I got lucky. There was a thick envelope in there, about

three thousand dollars thick, to be exact. I slipped it into my jacket pocket.

Ventuno had picked up his money on the Friday after what was left of Baby Lowen had been found. A pay-off for a job well done? Or film money? It wasn't long after then that he was being gutted. He'd never skipped town. He had no intention of skipping town. He had no reason to. I told myself he hadn't murdered Baby, but I wasn't sure. Judging from the handiwork, the same person had killed him as had killed Baby. On the other hand, maybe Leo was getting paid back for what he had done. An eye for an eye. A gut for a gut.

My thoughts were interrupted by the handcuffs pinging against the water pipe. Arnie was trying to pull himself loose.

"Cut that out!"

"You did it!" shouted Arnie.

"Shut up or I'll shut you up."

Arnie looked at me. His shoulders heaved as he looked up at me with a bleary gaze, then he seemed almost to shrink, his lip quivering. "Don't," he said. "Don't do that to me. Please. Please."

He'd somehow concluded I was the killer. I ruled myself out. I slid past Arnie, picked up the heel of my shoe, and limped up the stairs. It was time to call my old pals at the police department.

The sun was rising by the time I got to Bel Air. I parked on the street and dozed until I saw the maid fussing with the downstairs curtains. When she opened the door, her eyes told me how crummy I looked.

"Mr. and Mrs. Hitchcock have been in conference since seven," she said carefully.

"I don't want to interrupt," I said, sniffing, "but I believe it's important."

"And the subject is?"

"Murder."

She laughed awkwardly. "That's routine around here, sir."

I barely had time to glance in the hall mirror. I was still a raccoon with a swollen nose. I had added a five a.m. shadow, however. It was going to be hell to shave.

"Mr. and Mrs. Hitchcock will see you now."

In front of the neat bookshelves, Alma stood at Alfred's shoulder. There were several typed pages spread on the blotter with pencil marks all over them.

"You are up early, Mr. Slattery," said Alma.

"So are you two," I said.

"Coffee?" Hitchcock pointed toward a tray.

I wondered why they had nothing to say about my swollen and discolored face. Was this English properness or something? "I tanked up on quite a lot of police coffee last night, thank you." I must have glanced at Alma.

"Speak freely, Mr. Slattery," said Hitchcock. "Alma helps my thinking immensely. She's very good at plotting."

"Hitch is too kind. He exaggerates," she said, patting his shoulder.

"Well, the plot just took a strange turn," I said. "I found Leonardo Ventuno. He, too, was butchered."

"Oh, dear," said Alma.

I explained my little adventure with breaking and

entering, only I gave it to the Hitchcocks in the same order I'd given it to the police. The door was already forced and Arnie was inside.

"And so, you found the door open?" asked Hitchcock. There was no mistaking the amused inflection in his voice. He didn't believe me anymore than Captain Greene had.

Greene knew immediately I was lying, but winked at the deception. He was just happy to give Pete Cohn's chief muscle a hard time, and he knew in the long run it wouldn't make any difference. He didn't see any reason why Cohn would want Ventuno dead, either.

"There could be reasons of which we are not aware," said Alma.

"Indeed," said Hitchcock.

The police figured that Ventuno had been dead at least since the Friday that Baby Lowen was found, if we could accept that. The captain believed Arnie when he told them that Ventuno had been alive on Friday, when he came to the Knight Klub to have lunch with Pete Cohn. Arnie said he thought the visit was just social, and was silent about the envelope of money.

I didn't mention it to the cops, either. The envelope was lying hidden under the spare tire in my coupe. I knew Pete Cohn better not find out I had it.

"It does not exist, then," said Hitchcock. "Describe the crime scene for me."

I went through the details as closely as I could remember them. Alma grimaced several times while her husband listened impassively. He then asked me many questions about the look of things and items in the rooms.

"What sort of stuffed eagle was it?" asked Hitchcock.

"I don't know. A speckled one. A big one. Are you saying it means something?"

"Not particularly. But it's interesting, don't you think? I don't know why."

Alma smiled as if to say, "That's Al for you!"

After I told him all I had seen, I mentioned what the coroner had told Captain Greene. The killer had begun his disemboweling of Ventuno with a very clean cut in the groin.

"Ah!" said Hitchcock. "Now that is significant."

"What do you mean, Hitch?" Alma asked.

"Well, it is, isn't it?" he said. "They said the cuts were clean?"

"Yes. Like with a razor." I remembered the cut running from ear to ear on Ventuno's throat. I also remembered the body of a gangster killed in a barber's chair, and a husband who killed himself, or was killed by his foster daughter, with a straight razor. We never for sure figured that last one out.

"Or a scalpel," mused Hitchcock.

"The coroner said the cut was deep."

"Old scalpels were almost as long as bread knives," said Hitchcock. He raised his hand as if he held one in a stabbing position.

"The Ripper was thought to be a surgeon," said Alma.

I knew it was early, but they had lost me. "Are you saying a doctor is the killer?"

Hitchcock looked at me and settled back in his chair. "No."

"Well, what are you saying, for Pete's sake? There's never been any mention of a doctor."

Alma placed a hand on her husband's shoulder. I had been too forceful. "We are thinking out loud, Mr. Slattery. By the way, I hope you'll visit a physician."

"Thanks. I appreciate your concern."

"Icepacks," said Hitchcock indifferently. "All possibilities must be examined. A pity you didn't keep the cold cream jar."

"Huh? Well, I didn't think parts of Baby Lowen were good to keep around."

"The question then remains," Hitchcock said, "why was that ear sent to me?"

"Either Mr. Ventuno sent it and was saving the nose for himself," said Alma, "or it was sent to him."

"Did you notice any boxes or brown wrapping paper similar to what was used to send mine?" Hitchcock asked.

"I didn't really look for that," I said. "But I would have noticed."

Hitchcock turned the clock on his desk to see its face and began gathering the papers on the blotter into a file folder. "You must pursue other leads, then."

"Two murders," I said. "Isn't this a little out of our league?"

"Is it out of your league? Isn't this police work? Weren't you a detective?"

"Hey, these were sick crimes. This isn't some runaway daughter job."

Hitchcock looked at me almost contemptuously. "How will we know if we don't pursue it? Perhaps now that you've got a thick envelope of money, you'd rather withdraw."

I snarled. "A chunk of dirty money isn't my goal in life. Sir."

"I didn't think it was," he said calmly.

I rubbed my forehead and squeezed the bridge of my nose. "I'll talk to Walter Lamb and Whatizname Monaghan about her. But don't expect much. But after I go home and get some sleep."

He stood to leave. The maid announced that his limo was waiting. "Very good," he said. "Call Mrs. Robertson this afternoon. I will use my influence to have Mr. Lamb and Mr. Monaghan available for you. His name is Ward, by the way. And she can also get you an appointment with a studio doctor, if you like."

I didn't get up as he walked past me.

"Would you care for anything? Coffee? Tea?" asked Alma.

I thought about orange juice, but these were the kind of people who squeezed their own. I shook my head. "I don't want to be any trouble. Before I leave though, Mrs. Hitchcock, I wonder if you could tell me something."

"If I can, Mr. Slattery."

"Just what is Mr. Hitchcock's interest in these murders?"

"Why, Hitch is a genius, Mr. Slattery. I've known it since we met in 1923. Geniuses are interested in things."

It was the most obvious thing on earth to her.

CHAPTER
TWELVE

B y the time I got to my apartment, showered, and shaved, I caught that awful second wind that comes on and keeps you awake. In the 82nd Airborne and on the police, however, you learned to snatch rest whenever it was possible, even if you couldn't sleep. I lay on the bed with the pillow over my eyes and waited for the sandman to do his magic. I listened to the cars in the street and tried to put the memory of Ventuno's basement studio, the smell, and the buzzing of the flies out of my mind. The throbbing in my head wouldn't let me forget.

The day grew hotter, but I didn't open the window. The pillow grew damp with sweat from my forehead and began to feel good on the bruises. Eventually, I did fall asleep. Leo Ventuno approached me in front of Grauman's Egyptian

Theater. He was gray-skinned and his throat was slit, but he told me he would be better if I just bought a ticket from him. I did. I went inside. The screen was filled with Baby Lowen in an outfit like Yvonne DeCarlo's in *The Ten Commandments*. She reached out her hand and pulled me into the movie. I was Pharaoh's guard, but I was wearing my rent-a-cop uniform. She undressed and went down a set of stone steps into the Nile, enticing me to follow. She reached up as I came down, kissing my legs and hips and belly until I was all the way into the warm water. Our lips met, my eyes closed, and I could feel her breasts against my chest. When I opened my eyes, she was as gray as Leo had been and the Nile had turned to blood.

I woke up wrestling the pillow, then sat blinking, one hand gripping the metal headboard to steady me. My head pounded. A lot of people like to think that dreams are your brain's way of telling you something, so I tried to make sense of it. I got nowhere other than facing up to how long ago I'd been with a woman. I realized it was getting near a year.

Too long was the point. It might as well have been in a previous life. Maybe I should have married that French girl in 1945. Maybe I'd be picking grapes in the sun of Burgundy instead of scraping scum in the murk at the bottom of Los Angeles.

Peggy Robertson wasn't in her office when I called, but the woman who answered told me I had an appointment to meet Ward Monaghan at three in the commissary at Universal's television studios. Walter Lamb was still not answering.

Uh-oh, I thought.

Leo Ventuno had been looking for Baby because she resembled Kim Novak. Lamb, I figured, might have wanted a
model that resembled Novak. But Baby and now Ventuno
had turned up dead. I wondered whether Lamb's "periodic
illnesses" might have become permanent.

If I were still with the police, I asked myself, what would
I do?

Except in the simple cases in which the husband
shoots/stabs/beats wife (or vice versa) to death and tearfully
confesses, we used to sketch out possibilities on a chalkboard,
listing how the people involved connected with each other.

I found an old notepad in a kitchen drawer and tried it
out:

> –Christina Marie Lowen, "Baby," from
> Waterloo, father and former yahoo fiancé
> there (pick in paper), boyfriends (lots:
> Ventuno? Tex Grady. Pete Cohn? Prominent
> people?)

I tapped my pen on the table. Hitchcock? The master of
mystery was a mysterious man. Grace Kelly. Vera Miles. Kim
Novak. His stars ran to a type. At least one person thought
Baby resembled Novak. The blue blood of cops still ran in my
veins. I wasn't yet ready to accept that Hitchcock was merely
curious. On the other hand, I couldn't picture him filleting
two people. Not subtle enough. Not darkly funny enough.

Alma? Revenge? That was silly. The daughter Pat Hitchcock? Only in bad movies. Women don't kill this way. Not
unless they are raving lunatics. Obviously raving lunatics.
Those are the odds, anyway. Races may not always go to the

swift, nor battles to the strong, but it's smarter to bet as if they do.

> —*Pete Cohn* (would get Arnie to do it or maybe an
> out-of-town specialist)
> —*Smoky Tex* (beaters are usually remorseful and
> don't mutilate in a methodical way)
> —*Ventuno.* But who killed V?
> —*Walter Lamb* (where? Another victim?)
> —*the two cops* (who?)
> —*other lovers?* (Check who paid her higher rents.)

There were reasons to cross off almost everybody except the two cops (I still knew nothing about them), and the lovers I knew even less about.

Pete Cohn would be leaving some kind of message if he had someone killed the slow way, but I'd never seen a gangster use disemboweling. Cutting out the tongue. Breaking the legs. Neutering. Blinding. All sorts of methods, but you gotta draw the line somewhere.

Ventuno, I guessed, didn't murder Baby. The chances of two people going around doing this kind of butchering was mighty slim, but it was possible.

We had thought maybe Ventuno took a powder because he'd murdered Baby. What about the vanished painter? I figured three possibilities.

> 1) *Lamb was the killer.* He was connected to Ventuno and by him to Baby, though there was no proof he ever met her.
> 2) *Lamb was the third victim and we'd find another gruesome body.*

3) *Coincidence*. Lamb wasn't connected at all. It's
a small world and people bump into one
another.

That was always the third possibility in police work. In movies and books, coincidences are edited out, but in real life?

My stomach was grumbling and I was getting nowhere. Before I went for lunch, however, I made a list of things to check on. In complicated cases, the detectives shared the work this way. There was only me this time.

I ordered a creamed chipped beef sandwich at the diner on the corner. I know what you're thinking, but ex-soldiers get sentimental for the crap they've endured. It made me think of the way the victims were killed. A bayonet? Who was an ex-soldier in this case, other than me?

I got nowhere in this line of thought.

First, I went out to Paramount and asked about the tiny package delivered to Hitchcock's office. Nobody remembered anything. Packages came in all the time and nobody noticed who delivered them. Anyway, the gate supervisor told me, Mr. Hitchcock had already asked about it several days ago.

Next, I tried Walter Lamb's number and got nothing. I called Peggy Robertson to get his address, but she wasn't in. I got it from a Criss-Cross directory. It was getting to be two, and there wasn't time to drive down to his apartment in Venice, so I called Captain Greene. He had nothing new on either murder. A lot of stars and starlets and their various handlers—agents, producers, publicity departments—had made discreet inquiries about the contents of Ventuno's file cabinets, and there had already been a second attempted break-in out at Ventuno's studio, so the cops were removing the files to a safer location.

"It was that guy Fairfax," said Greene. "The one who our mutual friend said would bring you to him."

"Sig Fairfax?"

"Yeah."

"Did you arrest him?"

"No. He never even got inside."

"What was he after?"

"He tried to bribe our patrolman to let him look for some pictures."

"And the guy didn't take the bribe?"

"Imagine that," said Greene. "Policemen just aren't the same quality as us old guys."

"What pictures was he looking for?"

"Wouldn't say."

"You should have thrown him in the tank until he talked. It would have taken all of ten minutes. Maybe Fairfax is running errands for somebody who wanted Ventuno killed. Ever hear of blackmail?"

"Let's just say our inquiries haven't revealed any sign that Ventuno played that game."

"He was hardly an upstanding citizen."

"But the word gets out, you know."

I did know. Hollywood's shared secrets. A whisper here and there and suddenly your phone calls don't get returned. People don't invite you to things. The grapevine knows you can't be trusted and so your means of getting blackmail material vanishes.

"But that didn't mean Ventuno didn't have something on

someone who made a mistake before they were big," I said.

"I don't think Cohn would have let him do it," said Greene. "It might have interfered with Smoker Industries."

It made sense to me at that point, but who knows?

"Speaking of Cohn," said Greene. "Arnie's been released. Don't go down any dark alleys. He's a very unhappy gorilla. And they returned his forty-five to him."

The thought almost scared the pain in my face away.

Arnie wasn't the only unhappy man in Hollywood. When I got to the commissary at the television studios, the clerk at the cash register pointed to a bow-tied man who was red-faced, flexing his fingers, and staring at his sandwich as if he could toast it with his stare.

"Monaghan?" I asked. "Peggy Robertson—"

"I know, I know," he said. "Sit down."

"Thanks. What's the sandwich?"

"It's a bullshit sandwich. That's what they serve around here."

"Sounds par," I said.

"The guy's wearing a watch. So Apaches aren't supposed to wear watches! The extra should have known that, right? And then, cripes, the tattoo!"

"Tattoo?"

"The renegade drops in front of the camera and you can see 'Myrtle' and a Valentine's heart. This is *my* fault? The producer reams *me* out for an hour for this?"

"What show is this?" I asked.

"Believe me, you don't want to see it. It wouldn't matter if the Indians were wearing feather boas. You got a smoke?"

"Sorry, I'm out. I only smoke when I'm bored."

"I only smoke when I'm not bored, to keep from going nuts. This business!"

I set my hat on the table. "I'm told you ran into Baby Lowen when you were working the extras for *The Wrong Man.*"

"I didn't remember at first. I got a better memory for faces than names. But, yeah, the girl who was murdered. That happened once before."

"Huh?"

"Late forties. One of the girls I hired was run down by a coal truck on Sunset. She was a pretty one. I felt terrible."

"Baby?"

"The girl what got run down. Baby would have been a knockout in Podunk, kind of routine here."

"So she was used in *The Wrong Man?*"

"She got paid."

"Hitchcock met her?"

"Oh, no. There was some kind of delay. Vera Miles' hair, something like that. Then the scene dragged on and he never got to the extras. We sent them home. I remembered Baby Lowen because she asked me if she could meet Big Al."

"She called him Big Al?"

He looked exasperated. "I don't know what she called him."

"Did she meet him?"

"How would I know? I didn't introduce them. I sure didn't invite her back. Part of my job is to make sure the extras behave. I'll kill that bastard for his tattoo. 'Myrtle'!"

"So she was only an extra once?"

"A couple of times before the Hitchcock picture—crowd scenes and stuff—but not after that. When I tried to get her to go home she got mad and started yelling, so I didn't want her around anymore."

"Hitchcock see her yelling?"

"She was never on the sound stage."

I felt a little better. I remembered the way Hitchcock spoke to his wife, the way he listened to her, and the way they supposedly worked closely together. I was a little ashamed of suspecting him. "So that's all you know about her?"

"No, there was the business with John, too."

"John Ferren? You mean the art guy?"

"He called me and asked if I knew of a Kim Novak look-alike. The stand-in was too busy, and they needed a model."

"And you told them about Baby?"

"Actually, I came up with three girls. None of them could be called look-alikes, but they favored her. Ferren said that was good enough. The painting was only supposed to favor Novak. I tried to get hold of her and couldn't find her. I got the photographer's name off the portfolio."

"Leo Ventuno?"

"I don't— Say, isn't he—?"

"He was murdered, too."

"He was her photographer?"

"You don't read the papers too close, do you?" I said.

"Hey, listen," he said suddenly, "I've got this war movie coming up and I'm thinking you look kind of German and—"

"Thanks," I said, standing. I left him holding out his business card.

CHAPTER
THIRTEEN

I found a pay phone, but couldn't get anyone except associate producer Herbert Coleman's secretary. Hitchcock and Robertson were on a sound stage. Could I be transferred to John Ferren? She wasn't sure how to reach him.

I decided to wait until after dark to go to Lamb's. Didn't painters need sunlight? I drove to the studio. Hitchcock had kept me on the entry list, but I still ended up cooling my heels under the watchful eyes of a security guard outside the sound stage. "We'll check when the light goes off," he said firmly.

I paced. I watched a cluster of leggy women go by in bathing suits and tall, fruit-basket hats. Esther Williams kind of stuff, though I wasn't sure she worked for Paramount.

It was half an hour before the light went out. The guard checked with someone just inside the door. I waited another five minutes. The door opened and as I stepped in, I collided with a familiar man.

"Excuse me," I said. "My eyes are still—"

"That's all right," he said.

"Colonel Stewart," I said.

I blinked in the light. He looked weary, a man finished with a long day's work. "How are you?" he said. He seemed to be trying to recognize me. "Say, were you in Captain Taggert's crew?" he asked.

"I was in the Eighty-second," I said. "Name's Chess Slattery. I made sergeant by the end."

He smiled. "Really?" He extended his hand. "You boys did a lot of good work!"

"You guys did your share," I said. Stewart had been no phony baloney actor in uniform who made propaganda films and VD movies far from the shooting. He had talked the Army Air Corps into letting him in even though he was underweight. He had earned a pile of medals, including the Distinguished Service Cross and the Croix de Guerre.

"You kind of favored one of Taggert's crew, the tail gunner, I think." He lowered his eyes and nudged at a bottle cap on the floor. He was remembering. "It seems like a faraway time, doesn't it?" He didn't have to say anything more. He was one of us. Veterans hold on to things that others cannot imagine.

"A century ago," I said.

"You guys had it tougher than we did."

"I never heard James Stewart was a liar," I said.

He smiled. "That's kind of you to say so. Call me Jimmy and don't get Hollywood confused with the real world. How'd a guy from the Eighty-second end up here? Parachute stunts?"

"I'm working for Mr. Hitchcock," I said.

"Well, don't let him work you to death. He'll do good by you, if you do good by him. What do you do, by the way?"

I glanced around. Some people passing by were waving hi to him, but no one was in earshot. "I'm an investigator," I said.

"Really? Like Mike Hammer?"

"No, I'm just looking into something for him." I was being evasive, but I felt uncomfortable about it. This was James Stewart. He had put his life and movie career on the line to fly for us. You don't lie to a man like that. You don't lie to Mr. Smith.

"I read about it in the paper," Stewart said.

"The paper?"

"He's thinking about doing another true story, it said. You can't figure him out."

"This was in the paper?"

"The *Herald*, I think. You're Chester Slattery? It mentioned you."

I nodded. As Hitchcock had predicted, someone had gone babbling. Sig Fairfax? Captain Greene? One of the secretaries? It didn't matter. Shared secrets.

"He's interested in the Baby Lowen case."

"It's funny. I've never heard him say a nice thing about *The Wrong Man*. Maybe he wants to get it right next time. This picture's nothing like it. Pretty strange. A tough part for me."

"Did you ever meet Baby Lowen?"

He hesitated a moment, then began with a slight stammer. "To tell the truth, I did. I was talking with Hank the other day and he said, 'You know the girl that got murdered?' and I said 'Yes?' and he said she was at a party we both went to. I didn't remember right off."

"Hank?"

"Fonda. Henry Fonda. He was in *The Wrong Man,* you know. He recognized her from the papers. He said she jumped into the pool. I must have been inside at the time, getting a Seven-Up or something."

"Really? Whose party was this?"

He looked uncomfortable, as if he suddenly wasn't sure he should have been talking. Peggy Robertson had approached us.

"Mr. Slattery," Robertson said.

"I have been trying to find John Ferren," I said.

"He should be back at his office. Mr. Hitchcock will speak with you as soon as he is finished with Miss Novak."

"Thank you," I said. Next to the bed on the set, Hitchcock was smiling and talking to a very serious Kim Novak. She was wearing a satin bathrobe that glistened on every delicious curve on her body.

"Well," said Stewart, "I told Gloria I'd take her—Gloria's my wife—"

I put my hand on his sleeve. "I won't keep you, but you were saying about Baby Lowen—?"

Stewart leaned towards me. "Well, it wasn't much, really. I saw her once. At the Beverly Hills. It was a big thing. Wedding reception? Or something. One of the money people from

New York." Stewart lowered his voice. "You know, the kind of socialite who wants to go back and talk about who came to their party."

Hitchcock had a particularly sour expression at something Novak was saying. Stewart looked back. "She's got the jitters. I keep telling her to have confidence. Hitch likes her, but she doesn't think so." He smiled. "Of course, if I'd spent all day naked in bed surrounded by drooling men, I might be a bit jittery myself."

He turned back to me and regained his train of thought. "Anyway, Hank and I hung around the party just long enough to make sure our pictures were taken, then we went for Chinese."

"Do you remember if Lowen was with anybody?" I asked. "Who did she come with?"

Stewart shrugged. "I can't say I remember. She was wet when I saw her, so she was drawing a lot of attention from gentlemen who wanted to help her dry her clothes." He laughed. "Like Scottie in the movie. Everybody was very willing to help."

I didn't know who he meant by Scottie, but I let it pass. "Did Hank—Mr. Fonda—know her?"

"I don't think so. He recognized her from the picture in the paper, he said. He asked if that wasn't the girl who fell in the pool. That's all. I'll ask him, if you like."

"Thanks," I said.

"Well, I promised Gloria I'd take her to eat, if—"

"See you next week, Jimmy," said Hitchcock. He had sneaked up on us. I glanced around. Novak had slipped away.

"A pleasure meeting you," said Stewart.

"Likewise," I said.

Hitchcock tilted back his head, examining me. "You're star struck, Mr. Slattery."

"He's one of the best men in this town," I said.

"As an actor?"

"No, as a man."

"You see the best of yourself in him," said Hitchcock. "Everyone does."

Peggy Robertson came up to Hitchcock with a question. "I'll have to speak to you soon, Mr. Slattery," he said. "You might have to hurry to catch Mr. Ferren before he leaves. He'll be returning to his office."

"All I had to say is that I'm not getting anywhere," I confessed to Hitchcock. "I'm spinning wheels."

"In the middle of every production I feel exactly the same."

I quickly followed Peggy's directions along the studio streets and caught John Ferren. He was closing his office door and struggling with a large artist's portfolio.

"You're Ferren?" I asked.

"And I'm on my way home."

"Mr. Hitchcock sent me—"

"What now?" he sighed in exasperation. "I'm sorry," he said. "Couldn't you tell him you missed me? I was up half the night—"

"It's me that wants to talk to you, Mr. Ferren. I'm Chess Slattery."

"And—?"

"You were supposed to do a painting of Kim Novak several weeks ago."

"I did it," he said.

"Walter Lamb didn't do it?"

Ferren looked exasperated again. "What has he been saying now?"

"He hasn't been saying anything. It's just that he was looking for a woman who resembled Kim Novak."

"So he could do the Carlotta painting. Which he didn't do."

I didn't get it. "Who's Carlotta?"

"Carlotta. The woman who haunts Madeline. The woman who looks like Kim Novak."

"You mean in the movie?"

"What else would I mean?"

"So Lamb was supposed to do the painting?"

"No," said Ferren, "I was. But there was just too much for me to handle, so I asked Walt to do it on the QT."

"Why the QT?"

"A couple of years ago Walt was doing some matte painting at MGM. He got loaded and put something dirty in a cloud."

"Dirty?"

"A dick, okay? It was in the shape of clouds and they didn't notice it until the rushes."

I tried to picture this, but couldn't quite.

"He got canned. He went to Fox. There he fell asleep with a cigarette in his hand, ignited some wet paint, and nearly burned down a set."

"Two strikes and you're out?"

"That's it," said Ferren. "Since then he takes the cure every so many months, he comes back, finds something to do, falls off the wagon, and so on."

Periodic illnesses, as Hitchcock had said. "So why did you want him to paint the Carlotta painting?"

"Because I was too busy. Because I throw him a bone now and then. He's a quick painter when he's sober. He wasn't sober. I ended up doing it anyhow."

"And Baby Lowen?"

"I don't know anything about that, except that Walt won't work from a photograph. He wants a live model. I referred him to the extras people. He may have hired someone to use as a model for Novak. That's what he did in other situations. Is that all?"

I stepped in his way. "So how often do you take credit for Lamb's work?"

"Look, buddy," he said, "Walt wouldn't get any work if it got around. The execs would put the kibosh on both him and me. I let Hitchcock know, but he's no big mouth. Anyway, Walt thinks he's a *real* artist. He doesn't want anyone to know he does figurative work."

"Except when he needs a buck. So he's one of those guys who just throws paint at the canvas? Makes eight foot squares all one color?"

Ferren's expression must have been similar to that of the Roman nobleman who first spotted the Vandals rushing through the pass. "There's more to art than cows coming over a hill."

"Okay," I said. "I understand. It's art. I don't know what I like, even."

I looked out through the Venetian blinds for a moment. Ferren had completely confirmed everything Hitchcock had said. I don't know why it should have surprised me. On police work, you get used to the idea that everybody lies, always, whether they know it or not.

"I'm going home," said Ferren, walking past, "and have a cool beer."

"The phone book says Lamb lives in Venice. Is that so?"

"Yes," said Ferren over his shoulder, "but he isn't there."

"How do you know?" I asked.

"He called me today," he said. "He's taking the cure again."

CHAPTER
FOURTEEN

I recognized the name of the sanatorium. It was not far west of San Bernardino, at the end of the San Gabriel Mountains. It wasn't a particularly classy place, though it had had some classy clientele who found themselves on the skids and couldn't afford better.

The nurse who answered said she'd have to check if a Mr. Lamb was a guest, and, if he was, if he was receiving telephone calls. I had a momentary vision of Lamb in a strait jacket bouncing off his padded walls while being chased by a herd of vivid pink elephants.

There was a click, then a husky voice. "John?"

"Don't hang up. John Ferren told me where you are. I used his name to get you to answer."

"Hell, it's boring here. I'd talk to my aunt Matilda."

"My name is Chess Slattery. I'm interested in this painting you did for the Alfred Hitchcock picture."

"I never did it, man, and anybody who says I'd sell out like that is an asshole. If John said it, he's an asshole. He's sold out, anyway."

"Okay," I said, "I'm asking about the picture you were supposed to do. Look, it's nothing to me. Your secret is safe with me."

"There's no secret. I didn't do it. You're not calling about another job by any chance? Something else I'd never do?"

I rolled my eyes. It wasn't just the alcohol that had scrambled his brain. "When you're not doing these jobs for the studios, like the one you didn't do for the Hitchcock picture, you prefer to use a live model."

"Sure. Who wouldn't want to get Kim Novak undressed in his studio?" He cackled.

"Sure," I said, thinking of the way the robe had clung to her. "But you decided to use a look-alike?"

"If you can't get Veuve Clicquot, you drink Wild Irish Rose."

"So you met Baby Lowen?"

"Who?"

"The look-alike."

"I don't remember the names. There were three I tried to get. One had given up show biz for the glorious world of housewifing. Another was going to dance in a nightclub. The third I never found."

"How is that?"

"The phone number was wrong. I tried to get her through the photographer. He said he'd find her, but he wanted a commission. I said he could screw himself, then he said he'd do it anyway."

"This photographer, his name was Ventuno?"

"I don't know. It's all a little fuzzy. All this boredom. You should hear these people whining!"

"So why do you go there? Does it do you any good?"

"Three hots and a cot," he said. "And they let me paint."

"Sounds ideal," I said.

"It worked for Van Gogh. Maybe I'm not loony enough."

Just keep saucing it up. You'll get there. "Listen," I said, "if you think of anything else, give me a call."

"Man, I don't think," he said, "I *feeeellll*."

He hung up without taking the number.

On my way home I realized I would be passing within four blocks of the *Herald* building. Jimmy Stewart had mentioned reading about me in it. The story had gotten out just as Hitchcock predicted it would, but I didn't know exactly which one it was. In front of the building was a newsstand, but I figured I would get it free inside. I went to the rear of the lobby past the elevators and climbed the fire stairs to the third floor. Freddy Mancik's office was next to the door. I heard him down the hallway, yelling at someone. "They're not sure? How could they not recognize *her?* Her marrying that guy would be the biggest story of the year! You'll find it out, Johnson, or—"

I presumed he would say that Johnson would be back in classifieds or out on the street or something. A boy came down the corridor with a bundle of mail and dropped it on Mancik's desk. I nodded at him and waited until his back was to me to go into Freddy's office. The edition of the *Herald* on the corner of his desk was this morning's. I quickly found the page headed "THE WIDE SCREEN." Halfway down the second column was what I was looking for.

Hitchcock to Go Doc?

The great M. of S. has got PI Chester Slattery running down clues in the slaying of Baby Lowen, the winsome gamin from Kansas who was cleft from the nave to the chops and tossed behind the Bank of Pasadena.

Slattery, readers will recall, suspended the career of Western star Smoky Tex Grady with a well-placed knuckle sandwich. Tex is still having trouble breathing and may face surgery. Insiders say he keeps a six-gun in his glove compartment in case he sees the PI on the street.

Exasperated by the selfishness of stars Stewart, Novak, and Henry Jones, the M. of S. is at the end of his rope. "I'd do better without any actors at all," H. was overheard saying to cinematographer Bob Burks.

Will the Baby seduce the M. of S. away from original stories? Insiders say that the Hitch plans to find the killer. The last reel of "Hush, Little Baby" will reveal the murderer to a premiere audience wearing LAPD blue!

Freddy had always seemed harmless. You knew you couldn't count on a word of it, but it seemed fun. In the past, he had talked me into slipping up to his office with a couple of Photostats of arrest records the DA had suppressed. Movie stars, of course. Drunk driving. A statutory rape that was bought off and had really cranked me off.

I discovered it was a lot less fun if you were mentioned, even if you managed to be in an article with Jimmy Stewart, Kim Novak, and whoever Henry Jones was.

The discussion down the hallway was still going on, as if Freddy really cared about uncovering the truth. I took a peek at the mail in his in box. There was a manila envelope from Chicago, with "Open Immediately!" to the left below the address. I remembered Freddy offering me fifty bucks. The envelope was about the right size and weight to hold a calendar. I decided to commit a federal crime and carefully peeled back the flap.

I found Baby Lowen displayed nude above March 1956. She pouted like Clara Bow and squeezed her breasts together. She couldn't have been older than sixteen.

I tore her out and put the envelope back together with a stripe of paste. I pressed it flat with the blotter, then slid it under a pile of papers.

There was a noise in the hallway, but someone went into an office further along. A note scrawled on his blotter said, "Baby's black book. Where?" There were a couple of phone numbers. The one I recognized was the sanitarium where Lamb was drying out.

"What are you doing, Chess?" Freddy was in the doorway, his bald head gleaming.

"I was going to use your phone."

"Yeah?" he said, sharply puffing on his cigar. "There are pay phones on every floor. Who were you calling?"

"The M. of S.," I said.

"Yeah?" A lot of his anger seemed to vanish.

"Just a quick one. Haven't found out anything. Just to keep him posted."

Freddy moved around his desk. He was holding galleys in his ink-stained hand. "So what have you found out?"

I settled into the chair in front of the desk and dropped my hat on my knee. "I only know what I read in the papers, Freddy. It seems I'm a private eye, though I'm not. And who the hell is Henry Jones?"

"He's on that picture Hitchcock's making. He's appeared in a lot of stuff."

"Well, he's never done worse than showing up in your column. What are you saying that crappy stuff about Jimmy Stewart for?"

"You telling me he isn't a selfish swell-head like every other actor?"

"He fought for the country, Freddy, for your right to trash him. You know, Freddy, when I read 'The Wide Screen' I think maybe Hitler had a point."

"You mind if I quote you?"

"Keep me out of your paper, Freddy."

He puffed his cigar, blinking at his own smoke. "Or what? You break my nose it doesn't stop my career."

"Unfortunately. Who told you there was fighting on the set?"

"My sources are the best money can buy."

"You're making it all up. Don't bullshit me."

He shrugged. "You come here to insult me? I can go home. My wife'll do a better job."

"She knows you better." I stretched. "I was wondering if you had any leads on the black book."

He was startled but tried not to show it. "Black book?"

"Baby Lowen's. I heard she kept one. I heard it was interesting who was in it."

The wheels in Freddy's head were grinding frantically. "I'd give a lot for that book," he said. "Just so I could see it first. The police would get it right after."

"A lot of people are anxious about that black book."

"Like who? Like your pal, the M. of S.?"

"Oh, right, a sex scandal involving Hitch. You'd get laughed out of town. They'd bury your paper where it belongs."

"Who told you about the black book?" he asked.

I decided to bluff. "One of her landladies."

"The boozer," he said. "She called it an autograph book."

"Maybe it was an autograph book." I remembered that the landlady had also said that Baby wrote phone numbers on matchbooks. "But you figure to get more fireworks by calling it a black book."

Freddy shrugged. "You want the rats, you got to smoke 'em out of their tunnels." He tapped his pencil on the blotter. "A piece of advice, buddy: you get the thing before I do, you better get it to me."

"Now why would I do that?"

"Certain very tough guys with long guns are trying to get the book, I hear."

"Pete Cohn, eh?"

"And Arnie's already got a hard-on against you? If you pass it along to me, you might be able to walk the rest of your life."

"You mean you'd take a beating for me? Gee, Freddy, I appreciate that."

"Once it's public, it's worthless to Cohn for blackmail."

"Freddy, don't you ever get a little tired shoveling smudge?"

"Don't get righteous with me. One hand washes the other."

I knew he was referring to the copy of the statutory rape report I'd slipped him several years ago. He'd tried to pay me, but I refused it. An actor on a Disney picture had introduced a fourteen-year-old to adulthood. Suddenly she refused to testify. It was obvious her mother had been bought off. We couldn't do a thing to the prick, who was known for this kind of thing.

Freddy's smudging stuck good, and the guy was forced to move to Europe. He ended up as night manager to a hotel. That was one time I thought Freddy might really have a purpose in God's world.

"So who's washing your hand on this Hitchcock movie? You're getting bad info."

"My source is very close to the set."

"A tip, Freddy. Sig Fairfax is a liar. You bought a phony lead here."

I could tell from the way that his cigar drooped slightly that I had hit the target.

"So maybe Stewart and Novak are in love. What difference does it make? It helps your boss's picture, right?"

Freddy was never at a loss, but I felt pretty smart. Maybe I wasn't the worst private eye in the world.

CHAPTER
FIFTEEN

I telephoned Hitchcock to summarize what little I had uncovered, but he had already left for the day. I called his home. I got Alma, who said Hitch had just gotten in, but was waiting for an important call in ten minutes. Could I please call back later? When she checked with him, I could make him out in the background noise. He said I should drive out to Bel Air. I said I could summarize what I'd found out on the phone.

She told him this and he spoke louder. Maybe he was even snapping at her. Maybe I imagined it. I couldn't really hear. He wouldn't be used to not getting his way. She said he was suspicious about people listening in on his phone conversations. "I'll be out there in an hour," I said. "I'm going to make a few phone calls first."

It turned out to be fairly easy to get Edgar Lowen's phone number. He didn't really live in Waterloo, but in a small town outside of it called Dike.

The phone rang for some time. I gave him plenty of time to get in from slopping the hogs or whatever farmers did in late afternoon.

"Ed here," said the voice. He was the kind of man who shouted into a phone, as if it worked with a string and tin cans.

"Is this Mr. Edgar Lowen?" I asked.

"Yes. Who's speaking?"

"My name is Slattery, Chester Slattery. I'm investigating the death of your daughter." I was hoping he wouldn't be too curious about my credentials and assume I was still with homicide.

The line was silent for a while.

"Mr. Lowen?"

"My baby's dead. What's the point?"

"I'm sorry. I know this must be painful for you. We just don't want it to happen to anymore fathers."

"She was dead to me long before she ran off to California."

There was no hint of a choke in what he said. He was as cold as an Iowa wind in February.

"You called Christina 'Baby'?"

"Her name was Christina Marie. That's what I called her. She could have had anything she wanted, but first it was Chicago and then it was Hollywood. Who'll I leave my farm to now? My great-great grandfather settled this land seventy-five years ago."

"It's a sad thing," I said. "She was your only child?"

"Julia died giving birth to her. She was tainted when she was born. I told that to the other detective. Are you the some fellow they give it to when it ain't worth bothering with anymore? When nobody cares?"

"I care," I said.

"Well, I don't. What's the point? She did it to herself."

"No," I said. "The girl may have had her weaknesses, Mr. Lowen, but she didn't deserve what happened to her."

"The one I feel sorry for is Ray. He's letting his whole place go to seed. He believed in her. He forgave her. She ran off to Chicago with a truck driver when she was fifteen. After about three months he scraped her off like she was manure. She was living on the street doing God knows when she called. Ray talked me into taking her back, and she was a good girl for a while. But she started reading those movie magazines. She drove over to the outdoor theater in Waterloo. Then she disappeared one night after the movie. I knew what she'd done. Ray looked for her in Chicago but couldn't find her. But you know all this."

"It's good to hear it myself," I said. "Rather than just read it from notes. Maybe it's good for you to talk about it."

"'How sharper than a serpent's tooth,'" he said, "'is an ungrateful child.'"

"I understand how you feel."

"Do you? Have you got a daughter who jumped in bed with anything in pants?"

"She had her faults."

"You dance with the devil, you pay him."

"Um-hmm." What was I supposed to say? No, I didn't really understand. Who could? One thing you learn as a cop: you can sympathize, but people's sufferings are their own.

"My supper's getting cold," he said.

"I won't be much longer. I just wanted to know if you took any of her possessions back with you."

"Possessions? If she had any, somebody stole them. She didn't have anything. That's why she called."

"She called you?"

"She called Ray. She needed money. She wanted to borrow some. That's how we knew she was out there."

"She didn't call you."

"She knew what I'd say. I'm her father."

Maybe if he'd been a little less of his idea of a father, she wouldn't have been in Hollywood in the first place. "I'm not saying she had anything valuable," I said. "I'm just wondering if she had anything at all. Her clothes. Maybe an address book?"

"Somebody'd robbed that crummy cabin she lived in. Stuff was scattered. We didn't need a dress because the casket was going to be closed."

"You buried her naked?"

"It's the way God put her into the world. It's the way she wanted to live."

Thanks, Daddy, I thought. "You didn't by any chance notice an address book or an autograph book or anything she might have written things in."

"My supper's getting cold. I told you we didn't take anything. There wasn't anything."

"How about Mr. Cruikshank? Maybe he—?"

"Ray didn't take anything, either. He couldn't even find the engagement ring he paid seventy-five dollars for."

"Just two other things. Do you have Mr. Cruikshank's number?"

"He doesn't have a phone at home."

"No phone? It's 1957."

"You think he wants to talk about this?"

"No," I said, "but he might want to talk to somebody. Could you ask him to call me as soon as possible? Maybe you could ask if he has anything of Christina's?"

"He hasn't got anything."

"Please ask him."

"I don't expect to see him soon."

"Well," I said slowly, "when you do will you ask him. Will you ask him to call me, and only me, at the following number?"

"I don't know what the point is, but I will. Let me get a pencil."

"Thank you." Baby, Baby, Baby, I thought. And people thought you were nuts. Anybody who *didn't* run away from that place was nuts.

"Okay," he said.

I gave him my home number and told him if he didn't get me to keep trying. "If I don't hear from you, I'll check back in a week."

"I don't know if I'll see him by then. My last corn's coming in."

"That's fine, Mr. Lowen." There was one more thing I had thought I wanted to say, but I changed my mine. I was going to tell him that Baby had, for unknown reasons, taken out an insurance policy. I was going to send the death benefit to him. The three thousand that Pete Cohn had given to Leo Ventuno.

I changed my mind. Maybe I had no right to judge. Maybe I'd change my mind. Maybe I'd give it to Raymond Cruikshank. At least he seemed to miss her.

Or maybe I'd just give it to an old folks' homes or an orphans' society. Some place that showed a little bit of heart.

"Have a good evening, Mr. Lowen."

"I'll have to warm over my supper, now," he said. "It'll be dry."

On a chance Edgar Lowen had been putting me off, I asked directory assistance for Raymond Cruikshank's number. There was no listing for him. You had to wonder what would make Baby say yes to a proposal by a guy who didn't think he needed a telephone. The answer was obvious. To get away from home, even if it was only to the next farm. To grab hold of the only available man in the neighborhood. But then the truck driver showed up, and he smelled like diesel instead of pigs, and it might as well have been rose water.

I drove to Hitchcock's weighed down by all the sadness of this. Baby hadn't stood a chance since her mother died. Whatever gods ruled such things could have made her a movie star, but they didn't. And even if they had, like many of the glamorous, she wouldn't have stood a chance of being happy, anyway.

Alma told me her husband was still on the phone. I waited in the kitchen with a cup of tea turning cold while he had a long telephone conversation with someone at the studio.

He was petulant and impatient when he finally called me

in. He said there was still pressure about the title of the movie he wanted to call *Vertigo*. *"Face in the Shadow,"* he hmmphed. "There's nothing in the movie about shadows!"

He soon relaxed, however, as I told him the details of my investigation and he ruminated over the possibilities in what I was telling him. It had soon gotten dark and he had not yet turned on a light in his office.

"It seems to me," said Hitchcock pursing his lips, "that you might concentrate your investigations in two areas. First, the policemen who escorted Miss Lowen off the golf course remain unidentified."

I looked out the window, as if I expected them to reappear out of the bushes across the fairway.

"Secondly, there is the black book, or autograph book. Apparently it's not in Iowa! One can assume that it contains the names of people who might have a motive for wanting her dead. However, it seems to me that who is listed would be less important than whoever is most concerned about acquiring it."

"Isn't that fairly obvious?"

"You miss my point. Consciousness of guilt. The guiltiest party will go to the greatest lengths to get it. Your friend at that rag he calls a newspaper wants it, but it is merely a financial question with him. Similarly, Mr. Cohn is likely to be interested in the power it gives him over the names contained in it. But whoever killed her would have a far more compelling interest than merely business."

"Unless Cohn killed her."

"I trust your observation that gangsters wouldn't normally kill in such a dramatic fashion, except as a way of conveying a message."

"Make no mistake, sir. It's a way of looking at it, but Pete Cohn is capable of anything. We don't know that he didn't have a reason for mutilating her that way."

Hitchcock nodded. "Killing a person is generally not an easy thing, but for someone like Cohn it is easier and therefore less entertaining. Passion is the key to this crime. Certainly an insane passion, but one that may be rather commonplace. Love. Hate."

"Or a passionate devotion to the god Louie Lou-aye, who demands blondes be sacrificed." I crossed my legs. "You see what I mean. I'm stuck in the mud and my wheels are spinning."

"No, no. It is under our noses. It will be disappointing when we find the solution. It always is."

"What do you mean?"

"The pleasure is in the suspense, not in the solution."

"Is that why you end your movies so quickly?"

Judging from his look, I had gone too far. I wasn't the only person who'd ever said it, though.

"When Hamlet dies," he said, "the curtain should come down. There's no point in Fortinbras."

I didn't understand this remark—everybody knows who Hamlet is, sort of. But Fortinbras? It was the name Fortinbras that put me in my place.

"I'll take your word for it," I said.

"I am not a madman," said Hitchcock, "regardless of what I prefer people to believe. Find the two policemen."

"Yes, sir," I said. I had the distinct sense that he never allowed people to fail him.

CHAPTER
SIXTEEN

I walked out to my car thinking that a new approach was needed. Either I wasn't looking at the evidence right, or my way of getting at the truth was all wrong. I remembered that most of the homicide cases I'd worked as a police detective had been relatively straightforward. A guy kills his wife—or vice versa—with a kitchen weapon of choice: bread knife, cast iron skillet, rolling pin. Ten or fifteen minutes later he recognizes he's in trouble. He calls the police and tries to explain how it was her fault, while bursting into gut-wrenching tears over what he's done. Most of them confess and that's it.

The gangland kind of killing is quite the opposite: no one knows a thing and certainly no one confesses. Yet, if thug A is killed, everyone in town knows that thug B did it.

It's just you can't get anyone convicted unless they get really stupid and brag about it or keep the gun. What I'm saying is that most murders are a can of corn. The answer plops right in your lap.

The killings of Baby and Leo Ventuno, now these were the tough kind. No clear motive, but lots of possibles. The killer wasn't just angry. He had to be disturbed. Hitchcock had been right. There was some aspect of passion here. It wasn't enough just to kill her. It wasn't an accident of the kitchen variety. Ventuno and Lowen were connected, but not in a way that would make a killer do this twice.

I knew a lot about what this thing wasn't. I just didn't know what it was.

I considered simply staking out the police station during shift change. Maybe I could spot one of the two guys that had carried her off the golf course. It seemed like the kind of long shot you would play only if you had manpower and a city budget behind you.

But I wasn't a real cop anymore. What I needed was to do something strange, something police detectives wouldn't do. Something that would shake someone out of the tree they were hiding in.

I just didn't have the slightest idea what that would be.

My coupe was turning out of the driveway when I decided to try one more conventional thing, something I should have done right away.

Parking at the Bel Air Country Club clubhouse, I saw chauffeurs dropping off a number of tuxedoed men and their overdressed spouses for a wedding. I didn't fit in at all, especially with my face now shading off into a whole new palette of bruisey colors. I was stopped by the doorman throwing his arm across the opening.

"What's your business here?" he said.

"I wanted to get a membership application," I shot back.

"Can't you guys let the happy couple have their moment? Get moving."

"Who's getting hitched?"

"Like you don't know. Beat it."

"Hey," I smiled, "I really don't know. I'm not a reporter. I work for Mr. Hitchcock. I wanted to talk to whoever's in charge."

The doorman blinked. "He usually calls."

"Who?"

"Hitchcock. Why doesn't he put up something to deflect the balls?"

"So you heard about that?"

"Hey, people in glass houses shouldn't live next to golf courses."

"His house isn't glass."

"We're not talking Bobby Jones type skill out here. Some of these guys are lucky to hit the dirt in front of the tee."

He held the door for someone I thought was a muckety-muck with MGM. The guy avoided my eyes, though his date smiled at me with the same phony smile that all starlets perfect.

"Is there something special this time?" he asked me. He pointed at my face. "A golf ball didn't do that. Don't even try to claim that. The manager will send over a glazier right away."

I moved closer to him. The door traffic had slowed down.

I could hear a band playing Cuban music inside. "I'm not here about the window, and I wasn't hit by a ball. It's okay. What I was wondering about was two days before the last time his window was broken. Thursday, October 16."

"Last week plus some?"

"Yeah. Did any cops show up here that night?"

"Cops? Like city cops? Why would they? We've got our own security."

"But there was a girl on the eighteenth fairway about eight. She was taken away by two uniformed cops."

"Well, so I was told," said the doorman. "The manager was asking about it. Nobody knew anything about it."

"Why was he asking?"

"How would I know? Somebody asked him."

Hitchcock, probably, when he called about the window. I think he had said so.

"Is there anybody who might have seen something who didn't get asked?"

The doorman eyed me. "You've got a lot of questions. Is this worth my while?"

Everybody's seen the movies, I thought, they expected to be offered a sawbuck. "Hey, pal," I said, playing the role, "if you give me something useful, I'll give you a nice tip. Okay?"

"I don't mean anything. It's tough to get by as an actor."

"You mean you're not a real doorman?"

"Stuff yourself."

I touched his arm. "I was just joking."

"I have nothing to tell you anyway," he said. "The caddies were gone. It was a slow night. Saturdays generally are, but this was really slow. It had rained during the afternoon, so even the guys who hang around after golfing weren't here."

"Saturdays are slow."

"A lot of the members go out on the town on Saturdays. There were a few fellows in the bar. I didn't see anything on the course. I was out here twiddling my thumbs. That's all."

"The guys in the bar: members?"

He nodded.

"Who?"

"If I gave you their names I'd get in trouble."

Okay, okay, I thought. I took out my wallet and riffled through some of the papers in it. It was mostly papers, insulation to keep my dollar bills from rubbing against each other and making static. I plucked out a ten. He stuck it in his pocket without looking.

"Dr. Josiah Crestmont. Louis Carvalho. Chester Malinkrote. Paul Palango was with them, too. He got drunk, as usual, and threw up on the waitress's shoes."

"That's a new pick-up technique."

"He specializes in it."

"Why do you remember these guys?"

"They were the only ones. We were hoping to go home early. Crestmont drives a Rolls—he's a studio pill pusher. Carvalho and Malinkrote inherited their piles."

"Of money."

"Of money. So did Palango. He's from South America. Their cars were out here, along with a cream-colored Olds."

A bell went off in my head. "Who owns that?" I asked. The doorman shrugged. I remembered seeing a cream-colored Olds parked in front of the Knight Club. Sig

Fairfax had been driving one when he had met me coming out of my Pink job.

"A convertible Olds?"

"Yeah," said the doorman. There was cheering inside the building at the party, then applause.

"Is there a guy named Fairfax who is a member? Sig Fairfax?"

The doorman thought. "No. I don't think so." He checked the membership book locked in his station drawer. "No. But the name rings a bell. Maybe he came in here with somebody."

I waited for it to come to him.

He shook his head. "I don't know."

He leapt to his feet and opened the door for a late couple. Her dress had been painted on. In very thin paint.

I gave him another ten to give me the private numbers of the four men from the membership book, and made him promise that he would call me if he remembered why Sig Fairfax sounded familiar. Just like a private eye, I hinted there might be more money for him if he came up with anything good. He liked that. Life had become a movie.

An hour later, I had talked to all four men from the phone booth outside the party hall. I made up a cock and bull story about looking for a blonde who had walked off with a gold cigarette case. Neither Crestmont, Malinkrote, nor Carvalho had seen her. The curtains had been closed in the bar. Palango, if he had seen her, couldn't remember. He couldn't remember which night was Thursday, having drunk himself into lotus land on at least three evenings that week.

The waitress remembered nothing either, except Palango throwing up and getting virtually nothing for tips that night.

She was sure no one else was in the bar. I described Fairfax and it meant nothing to her.

I left the country club as some of the guests began to trickle out. I wound down into the city, driving slowly. I was nursing my second cup of industrial strength joe in a donut shop on Wilshire when I suddenly had an idea.

Come into my parlor, said the spider to the fly.

I climbed into another phone booth. It wasn't a police detective's idea. Maybe I was getting the hang of this.

CHAPTER
SEVENTEEN

A shot of bourbon took the edge off the donut shop coffee, and I slept good. I needed it for all I had done over the last few days and what might be coming.

At dawn, I telephoned Hitchcock and let him know what I was doing. He told me to be very careful and to check in with him later. There was a kind of excitement in his voice, which meant he thought I really had something, but it also made me think that he knew how far out on a limb I was climbing.

I got out of my apartment and drove to the closest newsstand. I waited until they dropped off the bundle of *Herald*s, then opened to "The Wide Screen," Freddy Mancik's cheesy column. I scanned down. This movie star was dating that movie star. This director was in love with that actress. Someone had tried to break into Errol Flynn's house, but his dog scared the burglar off. Raymond Burr was going to marry a geisha he'd met in Japan if her parents approved.

Amidst all this bullshit was *my* bullshit:

Cop Who Cold-Cocked Smoky Tex Has Lowen Black Book

Philandering husbands are quaking this morning as the rumors fly. Former police detective Chester Slattery, now employed as a technical consultant by no less than the M. of S. himself, is said (by those in the know) to have the lost black book of Baby Lowen, the not-so-innocent lamb recently found butchered.

Baby had secreted her tell-all address book beneath a loose board under her bed. If those planks could talk, there'd be a windfall for every divorce lawyer in town!

Studio chiefs are also quaking that his eminence the M. of S. can use Lowen's address book to dictate his own terms to them, even though his last movie, *The Wrong Man,* was a flop.

Word on the street is that Baby gave ratings to the romantic qualities of her many boyfriends, a source of pride for a few, but a humiliation for others. The Wide Screen promises to name names and provide more details as they are available.

I'd played Freddy like a fiddle, saying, "Suppose, just suppose, I should happen to have found Baby Lowen's black book under a floor board. What would it be worth to you?"

That's all I needed to say. He immediately began trying to pump me for anything in the book, then started bidding on it. He went pretty high, but I kept saying I wanted to see what the market would bear. Freddy finally said, "Slattery, I didn't think you were as low as the rest of us. I guess you've changed."

"I've got to make a living," I said. I didn't know whether Freddy meant what he was saying or merely trying to make me feel guilty. With Freddy you never knew whether he meant anything.

It felt particularly good to use him.

Sure, I should have known Freddy wouldn't leave it with what I was giving him. I had gotten what I wanted in the paper, but I wasn't thrilled with the extras. Hitchcock wouldn't be happy with that third paragraph, for sure. And where had Freddy come up with that ratings thing? Out of his disturbed mind? Or had he actually heard something? You never knew with Freddy. In the end I decided that whether it was true or not, it would probably help attract the mackerels.

I parked in the alley across from my apartment and read the rest of the *Herald* and part of the *Times*. I didn't have to wait long.

The first one who showed up was a young man. He loitered nervously by the front door for a while, looking both ways. He favored Howard Hughes in build and I thought if Hughes had met her, Baby would have had a contract. I recognized him after a few seconds. He had been delivering the mail in Freddy Mancik's office.

Okay, so Freddy was after the black book, or maybe this kid was trying to get a leg up in the journalism racket and one-up his boss. Either way shouldn't mean much to figuring out who killed her.

When he got enough courage he went into the hallway. He must have had lock picks or a master key because I soon saw shadows of him moving around my kitchen window.

I continued to wait. He was just coming out, trying to be casual, when a squad car barreled around the corner, siren whining. The boy started to run. Two cops chased him and knocked him down on the sidewalk. When they dragged him back to the car, Captain Greene came out of the back.

Greene watched as the officer yelled and threatened. All I could make out was, "So why were you running? Why?" Greene sent a man upstairs. Soon they were patting down the boy and tossed him in the back seat. People were gathering. One of them pointed towards the diner where I often ate breakfast.

Greene would have brought a *subpoena duces tecum* demanding the book from me. Sure, it would have been evidence in a murder case, but he had come personally to serve this one, meaning somebody important was quaking.

If Freddy sent the kid, he was just trying to save a buck.

Neither of them was who I was after.

The first baiting hadn't actually worked, but it showed I had hung the right worm on my line. The mackerels were biting.

With all this going on, I knew anybody else who wanted to toss my place would stay away for a while. I decided to drive away before I was spotted. I needed to go somewhere for a while to let the fish get really hungry.

I grabbed a carryout breakfast and drove towards the beach. The grease had congealed by the time I saw the Pacific Ocean, but I ate it anyway. Okay, I thought, let's see how much indigestion I can cause.

I got a couple of rolls of dimes from a bank that had just opened and went in a hardware store that had a telephone symbol on the window. The proprietor nodded without speaking. He was sorting nuts and bolts with the glazed exhaustion of a man condemned to do this for eternity. I took over the phone booth in the back and started with Pete Cohn.

"Yeah?" said a voice.

"Did I wake you?"

"Who the hell is this? It's nine thirty frigging o'clock!"

"Arnie," I said. "'Yeah' is no way to answer the phone. You need a lesson in manners."

"Is that you, Slattery? I'll give you a damn lesson."

"Give me Mr. Cohn, instead."

"He's asleep. Whatta you think?"

"Well, wake him up. Tell him to read the *Herald*. Maybe you ought to read it, too. I'll call you back later. Bye-bye."

I could hear him sputtering as I hung up.

Next, I dialed John Ferren's office. The studio operator put me through to him. "Have you read the *Herald*, Mr. Ferren?"

"That rag?"

"It reports a rumor that I have Baby Lowen's black book."

"Black book?"

"Names, notations about her hot nights with many gentlemen."

"Yeah? What's this got to do with me?"

"I thought maybe you'd like to buy a certain page of it."

"What? Why?"

"She mentions you."

"Huh? What does she say?"

"Aw, come on, you know . . ."

"I never even met the woman. Did Lamb tell her something about me?"

"Aw, come on, Ferren, we're over twenty-one here."

"You're nuts," he said, "and I'm busy."

He hung up.

Okay, I thought. I'll move him down the list. I continued to shotgun calls around town. Herbert Coleman (Hitchcock's associate producer) was more polite than Ferren, but he thought I was trying to trick some kind of scandal sheet story out of him and hung up with the words, "I never met the woman, ever. If you say so, I will see you in court. Good-bye, sir."

I tried to get Ward Monaghan, the extras wrangler, but he had stepped out for a moment, so I dialed the sanatorium where Walter Lamb was drying out. "Mr. Lamb is not available," said the nurse.

"Tell him it's John Ferren calling."

"Mr. Lamb is not available, Mr. Ferren," she repeated primly. "He checked himself out. It's outrageous."

"I'm sorry," I said.

"Do you know his whereabouts? He made a racket in the middle of the night, but before the attendants could get in. He went out through the window. Dr. Herschel says that he will be required to pay for the damage."

"Damage?"

"He broke out the metal grillwork."

"Over the windows?"

"How else would he get out? He's probably drinking himself to death in some dive at this very moment."

"I wouldn't doubt it," I said. When a man wants a drink, it can be a frightening thing.

I decided to let Cohn sweat it a bit longer and tried Walter Lamb's apartment. No answer. I tried Ward Monaghan again. When he answered I asked if he'd heard about Baby Lowen's black book.

"It's all over the studio," he said. "You got it?"

"I thought you'd be interested. Maybe you want to buy a page of it."

Monaghan was quiet for a while. "You know what? You're a son of a bitch, Slattery."

"Yeah? How's that?"

"Fifteen minutes in a dressing room," he said with a near moan. "That's all there was to it."

"When was this?"

"We were waiting for the street scene. It was the day the extras got sent home."

"From *The Wrong Man?*"

"She was trying to use me. I let her. Big deal, Slattery. If you think that's worth paying for, you've got another thought coming."

"Then you basically kept her out of the movies."

"She made a scene trying to get to Hitchcock. I can't have that kind of thing messing me up."

"So you used her and threw her away."

"Hey, *she* made the scene."

I didn't say anything. Sometimes if you're questioning somebody, they say more for the less you ask.

"So," he said, trying to sound casual, "what did she say about me? Something bad?"

"If you want to read it before everyone else in this town, you'll have to pay."

"For a dime I can read it in the papers," he said.

Once more I was hung up on. I thought about the conversation and decided he hadn't shown me any sign of guilt. That didn't mean he wasn't the murderer, though. I briefly toyed with the idea that if the killer was one of those mental types—and he had to be mental to do what he'd done to Baby and to Ventuno—then he might not even remember doing it.

Enough speculating, I thought. Back to the plan. Who else could I shake up? There were the other studios where Baby found occasional work. I needed to find out a bit more about her jobs after she came to town. The landlady had mentioned an inscription from Errol Flynn in Baby's autograph book. I'd have to get that number from somewhere. I might also see what Henry Fonda remembered about the party Jimmy Stewart had mentioned.

Hell, I thought, this is a big town. It wasn't like there were just a handful of suspects. There are eight million stories in the naked city.

I dialed Peggy Robertson's number. Another secretary answered and said that both Robertson and Hitchcock were on the sound stage, but she knew they were anxious to speak to me. Could I leave a number? One of them would call me back in fifteen minutes or less.

I waited, lost in my scattered thoughts.

"Hey, buddy—"

The phone booth door had opened as I was thinking and a tough-looking man stared down at me. He was huge and wearing farm overalls. On reflex, I reached for the gun under my jacket. I had it halfway drawn when the man's eyes went as round as a full moon.

"Jeez!" he said. "Never mind!"

"You startled me," I tried to explain. "Business calls."

He backed away quickly. "I'll find another one. Jeez!"

My heart stopped again. I snatched up the receiver and recognized the voice as Peggy Robertson's. "Hold for Hitch."

"Is this Mr. Slattery?" said the familiar voice. "You have something to tell me?"

"I'm trying to shake the rotten apple out of the tree. I'm sorry the article mentioned you. I had nothing to do with that."

"Sleeping with dogs gathers fleas. The point is whether you are having any success."

"The police are looking for me."

"Peggy tells me that Captain Greene telephoned me earlier."

"What did you tell him?"

"That I am quite busy with Miss Bel Geddes."

"The movie?"

"Of course the movie. I am on Sound Stage 5 at the moment. That is how I make a living, Mr. Slattery."

"Yes, sir," I said dryly. I told him that there were a few numbers I needed but couldn't easily get. Hitchcock said that usually he would go through Fonda's and Flynn's agent, but Peggy would arrange it for me in a couple of hours.

"About five I'm going to go back to my apartment and see who shows up. Anybody really interested will have tossed it by then and will know they need me to get the book. So they won't kill me until they're sure they can get it."

"Take all precautions," said Hitchcock.

"I didn't know you cared," I said. He hmmphed and hung up.

Okay, now, Pete Cohn time. I dialed the number.

"Slattery! Is that you? Where are you?" It was Cohn himself.

"How're you doing, Pete?"

"I hear you want to talk business."

"Why would I want to deal with you?"

"Because I can make it worth your while."

"How's that?"

"Look," said Cohn, "I don't want to talk on the phone. Why don't you come down to the Knight Klub—"

"What do you take me for? If anything happens to me, Photo- stats of Baby's book will go straight to three newspapers. But, all the same, I think Alexander Graham Bell did a wonderful thing inventing the telephone. What are you offering?"

"Look, Slattery," he said smoothly, "I got nothing against you. You're the kind of guy who can handle himself. You—" he hesitated as if looking away from the phone at someone "— put Arnie down without killing him. I never thought there was a man who could handle Arnie."

"Yeah, yeah. What's the deal?"

"We could work together on this. We could make a lot of money if we don't overplay our hand."

"*My* hand."

"But think what you could do with a partner."

"Partner? How could I trust you as a partner?"

Cohn laughed. "You don't know much about business, do you? Nobody who knows squat trusts his partner. Where's Roebuck these days? Just on the signs."

"You're hardly a catalog company, Pete."

"You need a good job, am I right? I can always use a guy like you. I can give you fringes like nobody. Arnie never buys a meal or a drink. You can hang around the club all night and take your pick. There's very cooperative pussy around me around the clock. What's your pleasure?"

"Sounds like Bali Hai. I just don't like the way you guys retire to the gutter with your brains on the curb."

"I'm a legitimate businessman," said Cohn flatly.

"Well, I'm not, and I figure you don't want what Baby says about you splashed around town."

"Are you trying to blackmail *me?*" Cohn laughed. "You're as dumb as you look, Slattery."

"Is that a threat? If anything happens to me, copies of the book are going to the three biggest newspapers in town."

"Ooh. You're making me wet myself." He spoke to someone else in his office. "He's trying to scare me." I could hear Arnie's rumbling laugh.

"Maybe I'll just turn the pages dealing with you over to the papers. That will make some of the others pay up quicker."

Cohn laughed again. "Okay, so what does she say? That she passed out from joy and exhaustion?"

"Don't flatter yourself." I suddenly had a new idea.

"Maybe you talk too much in bed. Maybe she overheard things that might make you want her dead."

Cohn paused. His voice was less self-assured. "I just did her a favor, that's all. The girl needed a favor. Like a lot of girls who just got to town. I introduced her to the right people. I let her hang around the club. If there's anything else in that diary, it's a lie."

"Did I say it was a diary? Who do you think it says you introduced her to?" I winced at saying this. I knew as it came out that it was too obvious.

But Cohn didn't call me on it. "Listen, Slattery," he said, "you do what you want. I just did the girl a favor and I'm trying to do you one. You come out to the club and we'll talk."

"Don't count on it," I said and hung up with the distinct feeling that something was wrong. Cohn hadn't seemed worried enough. Surely he'd have to think that Baby might, just might, have heard something that would cause him trouble. Even if the law couldn't touch him, his bosses in Las Vegas and New York wouldn't want publicity.

Trying to sort this out, I drummed my fingers on the phone booth shelf a little too long.

When I looked up, the hole at the business end of a police special stared at me.

CHAPTER EIGHTEEN

"**K**eep those hands high and clear," said the policeman through the door. He was young and nervous. His gun quivered. "On top of your head."

I quickly decided he wasn't one of the two in Hitchcock's drawing, but that didn't mean he wasn't in with them.

Using his billy club, he popped the door open. "Step out."

I moved very slowly. "What's the problem, officer?"

"You're carrying a gun?"

"Yes," I said. "I'm an investigator. I used to be a detective."

"Used to be?"

"I'm the guy who poked Smoky Tex Grady and got fired."

The cop squinted. "Slattery?" The man who had wanted the phone booth had drifted behind the television tube tester and peeked over the top as if he expected shooting.

"Chester Slattery. The guy there startled me. I grabbed my gun, but I didn't draw it out of the holster."

"Let me see some identification. He says you threatened him."

"I didn't."

He put the gun firm against my ribs and fished out my wallet. He checked several things that said who I was. "Look at the guy," I said. "He sneaked up and scared the bejesus out of me."

The policeman unfolded Hitchcock's drawing of the two cops who had carried Baby Lowen off the golf course. "What's this?"

"Do you recognize those guys?"

"No, who are they?" He handed it back.

"I was hoping you knew. They were patrolling the Bel Air Country Club area about a week ago."

"Don't get up there much. Why're you asking?"

"Just trying to find them." He fished out my Smith and Wesson, popped open the cylinder, and saw it wasn't loaded.

"He thought maybe you was a gangster or something."

"Too many nights at the drive-in," I said. When I looked, the big farmer was outside and stepping away from the front of the store.

"You have cartridges?"

"In the car." I didn't tell him about my ankle piece.

"Sorry." He holstered his gun and handed mine back. "So, did Smoky Tex put up a good fight or did you really take him out with one punch?"

"If he ever fights a hundred and twenty pound girl, I'd take odds on the girl."

"He had two wives he bea' the snot outta, I heard. Well, sorry to bother you, I'll smooth it with the—" He scanned the front of the store. "Hey, where'd he go?"

The proprietor, who stepped out from behind the nail bins, pointed up the street. "Chickened out, I guess."

The proprietor was sweating, but he also had the happy look of someone who would now have something to tell his family.

The iodine smell of salt water came up the street from the ocean. Maybe if the wind blew hard enough, if we got a typhoon the size of Nevada, it could sanitize the whole city.

I saw the cop at the next intersection, looking both ways and scratching his head. I tipped my hat, he shrugged, and I went to my car. My plan was to kill a little more time until Robertson had some more numbers. I would try those and see what I got—I expected nothing—then sit up in my apartment and see who turned up.

I wasn't that far from Walter Lamb's address in Venice, so I drove over there. Some drunks like to get immobilized in a bar, others find a nice womb in the bushes, but most like to hole up at home, sweet home where they can be alone with the bottle they love.

The address turned out to be a cottage on the beach that looked like it hadn't been painted since Drake claimed California for Elizabeth I. The nearby construction of a pink motel hinted at the future for this row of buildings: bulldozers, then shops selling lamps made out of sea shells. Some sand had drifted up around Lamb's porch, but there were smoothed tracks going up to his screen door.

That wasn't what made me load my Smith and Wesson. Inside the screen I could see the fresh gleam of wood on the front door. Somebody had kicked it in. I told myself it could have been Lamb, drunk and without his keys. I had the feeling it was more.

I hid the gun in my jacket pocket, keeping my finger on the trigger and the nose forward. I opened the rickety picket gate and tipped my hat at two old men sitting on the next-door porch. I walked toward the house as outwardly calm as an encyclopedia salesman, but alert for any movement inside.

"Mr. Lamb?" I rapped on the rusty screen door. The front door was almost closed. I could make out nothing inside. I stood on tiptoe and tried to look through the row of little windows on the top of the door. They were too dirty.

I banged on the screen door again. "Mr. Lamb? Hey, Lamb!"

Shooting a quick smile at the old men next door, I took a firm grip on my pistol, jerked open the screen door, and stepped inside.

In the front, a small living area contained a settee, a lamp, and a couple of tables. A rocking chair with an ottoman sat in front of a small gas heater. Everything seemed in its normal place except for the books. They had been pulled from the bookcase and were scattered on the floor.

The air was stale and there was a stink, but it wasn't the smell I had braced myself for. It wasn't *that* smell.

"Mr. Lamb?" The whoosh of a sea wind against the house was the only answer.

In the kitchen-dinette, the cabinets had all been opened and some things pulled out. Lamb had several plates and an odd assortment of flatware. There were spots of different colored paints on the spigot handles, on the coffee mugs, and here and there on the counter.

The refrigerator door was open about an inch and it hummed loudly, trying heroically to do a job it wasn't built for. I held my breath, expecting anything. A bottle of milk had separated. Part of a roasted chicken squirmed with maggots. A furry mold covered a bowl of who-knows-what like a muff hiding a rich woman's liver spots.

Now I knew why the house smelled bad, but, again, at least it wasn't *that* smell.

In the corridor past the kitchen, there was a bathroom with a dripping faucet and a bedroom with a rumpled bed. Fingerprints and blobs of red, blue, and white marked the doorknobs, the doorframes, the sheets, and walls. The wooden floor had a rainbow of partial footprints that led out to Lamb's studio, an enclosed porch. The ratty curtains had been pulled, coloring the light a dirty orange.

Some canvas rolls had been tossed around. A coffee can had been knocked over long enough ago that the brushes that had tumbled from it had hardened. A stack of large paintings lay flat on the floor, knocked over from the wall they had been propped against.

I lifted the top one. It was a large red thing with a single green stripe across the middle. The one under it was a darker red with a blue stripe. The ones under that were similar. They might have been starts at something, or they might have been finished. Who can tell these days?

All I knew was that the paint was still wet. I'd gotten some on my fingers. I looked for a rag on the worktable, but before I found one I noticed a canvas torn on its frame, sitting at an angle between the table and the wall. Lifting it out, I saw it had been slit upward and then across. The squares fell into place when I turned it around. It was a picture of a woman. A blonde.

Baby Lowen?

The painting was unfinished. There was still some pencil sketching in the thigh muscles and breasts, though the head was almost complete. She was standing in a pose like the famous picture of Marilyn Monroe over the subway grate in *The Seven Year Itch*.

It could have been Baby Lowen. The hair wasn't right, but if you were thinking Baby Lowen, you'd see it as her. One cut went straight across the throat. The other began between her legs and split her from the crotch to the throat.

That was how Baby had been sliced open.

Had Lamb lied about meeting Baby?

I stared at the head and still couldn't be sure it was Baby. Maybe it was Baby being transformed into Kim Novak or Vera Miles or Marilyn Monroe. The pose didn't look like anything that was supposed to become the Carlotta painting for *Vertigo*.

Who was this supposed to be? "Art aren't what it used to be, Magee," I said out loud. I tore off the head section, rolled it up, and took it with me.

I did one more turn around the inside of the cottage, saw nothing else interesting, then went outside. The two old men were still rocking on the porch. They were closely watching a body builder lurch along the water's edge in some imitation of running.

"Hey," I shouted, "you guys seen Walter Lamb?"

"What's it to you?"

"He told me to come by."

"You went in. He's not home?"

"He left the door open."

"Haven't seen him."

"When's the last time you saw him?"

"What's it to you?"

I tipped my hat. "Thanks. You've been a big help."

"And we're still not selling, so forget it!" They went back to watching the runner.

Enjoy the bulldozers, you old bastard, I thought.

I opened the picket gate and stood for a moment breathing the Pacific air. I understood why you'd want to keep a place on the shore like this, no matter how run down. But the developers always win, one way or another. They take the land, use it for their purposes, and throw it away.

This beach. Baby Lowen. They weren't the same in every way. Baby Lowen hadn't been worth developing.

I was still sorting those thoughts when I opened Lamb's mailbox. Sand had blown around the edges of the door and piled against the package and the bills wedged against it.

I shielded the mailbox against the old men's view as I tugged the package out and held it against my belly. Sand fell on my shoes. A postcard stamped "FINAL NOTICE" in red fell and blew through the pickets.

I didn't try to catch it. The package meant it would never be paid.

CHAPTER
NINETEEN

I drove back into town, the package under my front seat. I didn't need to open it to know what it was. All I knew was that I needed to get rid of it before I had my expected run-in with Captain Greene or one of his men. All I needed was to be caught with a piece of Baby. I knew too damned well that when a case became embarrassing there's a tendency to hang it on the first convenient bozo.

And, boy, I thought, would I be convenient! I had found Ventuno's body. I had been all over town asking questions about Baby. I was "known to be violent," as we used to say, having assaulted Smoky Tex Grady. And so forth and so on. Hell, I'd be tempted to hang all this on myself if I was still a cop.

You need friends to pull you out of stew pots like that,

and Hitchcock might be all I had. But I didn't know him well enough to know whether he would go out on a limb for me. I had the feeling he would—actually, I was pretty convinced—but I also knew that instinct is way overrated.

I pulled into a gas station and tried to get him on the phone. The secretary said both he and Peggy were unavailable. She said that Peggy had those numbers I had wanted, but needed to know where she could call. I'd try later, I said, and then added that I wanted Walter Lamb located, or any sort of lead to where he was.

"I'll convey your message," said the girl.

Driving to avoid the main streets as much as possible, I made a mental list of places mokes I had arrested had hidden things like murder weapons or swag. Wrapped in oilcloth and sunk in the toilet tank. Under floorboards. Buried in the backyard. In a birdhouse. Of course, we'd found all of these, except the leather pouch in a hole in a tree.

I laughed at the last thought. Bees had nested right on the stolen jewelry. The suspect had a very bad day when he tried to get it out. He capped off his trip to the doctor's by meeting me at his fence's.

If I rented a post office box or a safety deposit box I might be identified too easily later. Check it at the bus station?

There was the old movie dodge of mailing the package to myself. Philip Marlowe and Sam Spade and a legion of other PIs had all done this. This would be a novelty in this case. None of the three packages had actually been mailed before. Hitchcock's was delivered to his office at the studio. Neither Ventuno's nor Lamb's had postmarks.

But I worried the package might show up too soon. It might be delivered in twenty-four hours, about the time I least wanted it.

Hot potato, hot potato: I was beginning to feel like I had picked up a bomb, was riding around on top of it, and had no way to get rid of it.

It was then I spotted one of the Los Angeles area's least likely business successes: a bookstore. Not only was no one likely to look in one, certainly no cop was likely even to think of one.

In the dusty back of the store were thick old technical books, long outdated. The lower shelf was just the right height off the linoleum.

Breathing a little easier, I fortified myself with a cheese-burger and telephoned the sanitarium. No, they had not heard from Mr. Lamb, but they were very anxious to find him.

I also tried Hitchcock again. No, he was not available. No, they had not been able to locate Mr. Lamb. Could I leave a location where I could be reached? "Mr. Hitchcock knows where to reach me later," I said. "I'll be there in about an hour."

They were waiting, as I expected: one on each corner, smoking and trying to look casual, as if I wouldn't recognize that cop way of scanning the street. One of them was named Dixon, I remembered. The other was young and big enough to snack on diesel engines. One for muscle, one who can re-member what the suspect says while the muscle pulps him.

What surprised me as I parked was the doors popping open on the Chrysler across the street. Captain Greene himself. Well, this was going to be a party!

The two detectives hurried up from each direction. Greene came up behind me as I pretended to fiddle with my keys.

"Hey, Captain," I said, "how's kicks?"

"I'll kick you if you don't give me that address book," he said.

"Right here on the street?"

"On the street. In a cell. You name it."

"We could step up to my apartment, if you promise to behave."

"This isn't funny, Chess."

"Am I laughing?"

The big guy shoved me. "G'wan," he said.

"Take it easy," I said. I opened the door to climb the stairs. I already knew part of what I was trying to find out. The apartment had been searched earlier. They knew the book wasn't up there. If they'd wanted to torture the location out of me, they would have taken me to the station, or more likely to a nice scenic location far from prying eyes. My reading of this was that they wanted the book, but Greene, at least, had no personal stake in its contents. He was still playing with the stops in.

I unlocked the door. My sofa was standing upright on its end, the thin fabric underneath had been slit to get at the springs. The drawers of the end tables had been pulled out and overturned. All of the kitchenette cabinets were open, my closets ransacked. My mattress leaned against the wall and the springs sat off the frame. Even the lid of the toilet tank had been lifted off. It sat in two pieces on the bottom of the bathtub.

I charged back from my bedroom. "What the hell is this? Did this elephant do all this or did somebody have to explain it to him?"

"Take it easy," said Greene. "My men wouldn't toss your place like this."

"Oh? So you tidied up and declared open house for the neighborhood after that?"

"Watch it," said the big guy. He shoved me back so hard I backed into my own refrigerator. The door swung and an egg rolled out, smashing on the floor.

"You could have at least closed the damn Frigidaire," I said. "Damn!"

"I had to go back to the office, but Hames and Archer wouldn't have done this," said Greene. "You know Hames and Archer."

"Archer? The son-of-a-bitch hates me!"

"Well, it *was* his wife," said Dixon, the smaller detective.

"His *ex*-wife," I said, "and I only went out with her twice, to the movies."

"He's Catholic," said Dixon.

"That's all pussy under the bridge," said Greene. "Give me the book, and I'll personally order him to clean the place."

"It wasn't pussy under anything," I said, "and what's more, I don't have any book."

"Come off it. Everybody in town knows you do."

"Then everybody knows wrong. I don't even know if there is a book."

"That isn't what I read in the papers."

I shook my head. "Freddy Mancik, now there's a good source of evidence."

"It isn't just Freddy. Other papers are reporting it, too."

"Then they stole it from him. I don't even know there is a black book. I heard she kept an autograph book, but that's all I know. I don't even know if that's true."

Greene and the two detectives eyed me in that semi-amused cop way that means, "Yeah? I once saw a pig fly, myself." It was strange to be on the other end of that look, especially if you knew you were telling the truth and the pig *did* fly.

"Look," said Greene, "if I find out you're pulling a fast one, a little greedy maneuver to get even with some of those studio mokes who—"

"Save your breath," I said. "I haven't got it. I don't know where it is. If I did have it, yeah, I'd sell it page by page, a thousand bucks a page."

"So you know it's got hot stuff in it?"

I grinned. "It must. Everybody wants it, don't they? If you want to arrest me for withholding evidence, then do it. If not, I've got some housekeeping to do."

Greene stared at me for several seconds. I could hear Dixon breathing. I didn't want him to be sure I didn't have it, but I couldn't spend all night being questioned, either. I was continuing to gamble on the notion that Greene wasn't involved in the murders or in any part of Baby Lowen's life. Or that if he was, he would more likely set a couple of his trusted bulldogs to watch me until I led them to the book.

"Okay," he finally said. "I'll let you pass on this, Slattery. But if I get the slightest indication—"

"I know," I said. "I know."

Dixon looked a little disappointed. I think he wanted to see the moose in action.

"I'll tell Archer he got out of hand," said Greene.

"Don't bother," I said. "He's a much happier man believing she screwed me and the milkman and everybody else."

They left without saying anything else. I watched from the window as they talked by Greene's car. Greene left, then the two of them walked to a car parked some way down. I didn't really believe they were leaving, but I would recognize Dixon if he staked me out, and the moose was too obvious. Greene would try to put in a cop I didn't know. Probably he was already out there, or soon would be.

I watched a man in a painter's coveralls walk by. Two teenagers played pitch penny. A man in a double-breasted suit argued with a woman. I didn't see anyone on the roof opposite, but that didn't mean no one was up there, back against a chimney, nursing a warm bottle of Nehi.

My church key was almost as lost as Baby's autograph book, but I finally found it and popped open my last Pabst. I set down my sofa, turned out the lights, and settled back to wait. The beer got warm, the night grew deeper. Every once in a while I crept up to the window. I saw nothing new opposite me until ten-thirty, when a couple came out of the roof door. The man pointed at a few stars until the girl threw herself against him. It was a long kiss. I'd kind of wished I'd timed it. Actually, I kind of wished I was on the receiving end.

About eleven, a man began to loiter just inside the alley to my left. He was still there at eleven-thirty. He'd either been stood up or he was Greene's man, I figured, though I never caught him looking directly up at my window. I dozed a while. I checked outside again. He wasn't there. No, he had only stepped back into the alley, just out of sight. It was twelve-twenty, now. Someone stopped to talk with him for about five minutes. The other man left. I had expected him to relieve the other guy.

My phone rang. It sounded like a machine gun in the quiet. I jumped up, knocking over my warm beer, and pulling my pistol. My heart pounded.

"Hello?"

"Good evening." There was no mistaking the voice.

"How's the movie business?"

"Frightful," he said. "Shooting the movie is the most dreadful bore."

"Looking at Kim Novak in a bathrobe is boring?"

"No," said Hitchcock, "but filming her in a bathrobe allows for little enjoyment. How is the bait?"

"Just fine, thank you. I've been rousted by Captain Greene and a couple of dicks, but I don't think they're all that interested."

"Cat and mouse?"

"Maybe, but Greene is more of a dog than a cat. I'm not sure he believes what he read in the *Herald.*"

Hitchcock hmmphed. "No sensible person does. The question is, who can't afford to take a chance it is false."

"Listen," I said, "the plot thickens. I found—" I suddenly thought that someone might be listening in. It was paranoid, maybe, but people *were* out to get me. "I found something of interest to us. A package was delivered to Walter Lamb."

He instantly picked up on my caution. "A small one, I assume. With another—ahem—piece of the puzzle?"

The image of Baby's mutilated face made me wince. "Yes," I said, "another piece."

"Which part?"

"Excuse me?"

"Which part of the puzzle?"

"I didn't actually open it. It was wrapped identically. It was the same size. I assumed it was part of the game."

"You should never assume," said Hitchcock.

The remark ticked me off. "Yes, Mr. Holmes. What difference does it make which part it is?"

"That's impossible to know at this point, isn't it?"

I rolled my eyes. "Has anybody located Walter Lamb?"

"He seems to have vanished, but, understand, he frequently does so. John is not alarmed. Walter frequently tries to live up to the ambitions of the abstract expressionist school by behaving erratically."

"John Ferren, you mean?"

"He knows Walter better than any of us."

"Don't you think there is reason to be alarmed?"

Hitchcock was silent for several seconds. I could hear him breathing. "Possibly," he said.

"Are you assuming I'm assuming again?"

"The package, you assume, marks one for a nasty end."
"Well?"

"Two of the three recipients," said Hitchcock, "are not known to have met their ends."

"All things considered, I wouldn't go down any dark alleys," I said.

"Which reminds me—" said Hitchcock.

A noise made me pull the receiver away from my ear. It wasn't a loud noise, just a squeak. I glanced out the window, although I was sure I had heard it towards the back of the apartment. The man by the alley had disappeared. The street and roof were empty.

Hitchcock's voice squawked from the receiver. I couldn't make out what he was saying. I said, "I'll call you back," and hung up.

I moved away from the window so I wouldn't be silhouetted against it. I pulled my Smith and Wesson and eased up to the corner. My bedroom door was half closed.

I watched and listened. Maybe the noise was just the neighbors upstairs getting amorous.

The door moved.

Not a lot, just enough to squeak the old hinges.

A breeze, I thought.

But I never opened the bedroom window. The fire escape was too convenient, and anyway, I'd thought it was painted shut.

I listened intently and thought I could make out night sounds coming from behind the door, but I wasn't sure. The window behind me was still open and somebody was shouting from a passing car.

"Hello!" I shouted. "Anybody there?"

A dog barked far in the distance. A truck rumbled by on a nearby street.

"Show yourself and I won't shoot."

The dog barked again.

"Speak up or I'll blow you apart."

Again, nothing. Could the wind from the front move that door? It was possible, I supposed. I waited probably a full five minutes, feeling the hairs centipede up and down my back, trying to decide if the presence I felt could be the result of one overly warm beer.

I went around the corner, flattening myself against the wall to make myself a narrower target. It took three hundred years to reach the door, and for part of that time I was back in a post office in Brittany trying to find the Stormtroopers who were hiding inside.

I shoved the door with my foot. My mattress still leaned against the wall. My dresser was still pulled apart and my socks and underwear still scattered.

When I looked at the window, it, too, looked untouched. I'd just had time to think I was imagining things when I saw one of the windowpanes, sitting on top of the radiator. Somebody had worked it loose to reach the latch.

A shadow came at me from the side. There was a red flash of pain and I could no longer feel the gun in my hand. I brought my left fist around hard, catching nothing but air. A fist drove hard into my midsection and suddenly there was no air anywhere.

I was spinning, no, being spun by the arm. My legs were out from under me and I was dropping into an open pit.

I flailed, but the fight was nearly over. I had landed hard on my rear. A leg was wrapped around my hips. A hand pushed against my temple. My throat was in the steel bend of an arm. I clawed back with both hands and felt wool or hair. The arm grew tighter around my neck. I couldn't breathe.

"Easy," said the man. "Easy. I don't want to hurt you."

The voice was familiar. Where had I heard it? I relaxed a little, to lull him into thinking he had won. Which he had.

"I want the address book," he said.

I gasped for air. "Not here," I said.

I blinked and saw the man was wearing black trousers and combat boots. His leg wasn't all that large, and yet I was as helpless as a bug on a pin. He could break my neck, choke me to death: his arms were like steel.

"Where is it?"

"I have to show you."

"Where?"

He tightened up. My eyes were going to pop. I went limp and he let up. I gagged and coughed and wheezed.

"It's hid," I managed to say. "Hidden." I panted. "I'll have to show you."

He twitched to threaten me. "Tell me."

"Okay! Okay! Just let me catch my breath!"

"Now!"

"Trailways," I said. "The bus station."

"In a locker?"

I nodded.

"Which one?"

"One twenty-five. At the north end."

He squeezed my throat again. "I don't believe you."

"I swear! I swear!" I was thinking about the kitchen, but decided a knife—even if I could get my hands on one—would be useless against this guy. He was smaller than I was, but he was a badger. Probably a professional. Maybe my ankle piece?

"I hid the key in my shoe," I said quickly.

"Kick it off."

"It has a trick heel."

"Kick it off!"

"It's like a Chinese box. You've got to push two places and pull–"

The chop to the side of my neck came out of nowhere and like a thousand volts, it straightened me out flat, gasping for air.

The man was up, tugging at my shoe. I blinked and the light from the street light filtering through the window showed him to be a small, pudgy guy, wearing a black nylon mask covering everything but his eyes and a black Eisenhower jacket without markings. A surplus O. S. S. outfit? The O. S. S. had become the CIA in 1947. His clothes strained to hold him. Either he'd bought them small or he'd put on weight since he first got them.

He jerked my shoe, banging my head back against the floor. My pants leg slid and he spotted the tiny holster on my ankle.

"You son of a bitch!" He was angry and exasperated. "I don't want to hurt you! I just want the damned book!"

He tore the little pistol off my shank and banged my shoe against the bathroom doorframe until it broke off. I could hear his breathing.

"Don't you understand?" he pleaded. "I don't care whether you get hurt, but I'm not going to let others get hurt. If I have to kill you, I'm not going to let others get hurt!"

He pushed the gun hard against my knee.

"Do you know what it's like to take one in the knee?"

The fog blew off and my brain suddenly cleared at the

prospect. The pain is said to be unbearable. And you limp forever.

"Don't do it," I said. "I have to explain."

The man jerked at a pounding on the door and I grimaced, waiting for the pain from the shot. But he hadn't shot. He had lifted the gun and turned toward the sound.

I kicked, as hard as I could, and caught him with my shin on the side of his face. With a flash of light the gun popped and he flew backwards, sliding back into the kitchen.

The pounding on the door had turned into a thump and the door sprang open with a crack. Two cops in uniform smashed into the living room. I could see Army Colt .45s stretched in front of them silhouetted against the front window.

That is wrong, I thought. This is a nightmare. Cops don't carry Army Colts.

CHAPTER
TWENTY

lattery?" said a voice. "Police. You're to come with us."

A flashlight swept the living room, then blinded me as I climbed to my feet in the hallway.

"Identify yourself," I said.

"We're officers. Come with us."

"Am I glad to see you! What was your name again?"

"Smith," said the voice. "Joe Smith."

I rolled back toward the bedroom and dived. The .45 made a deafening *WHUMP!* three times as it ripped holes in the swinging door. I sucked in a deep breath to dive through the open window onto the fire escape, then I heard a wet grunt and the crack of an arm breaking. Another shot went off, and someone hit the floor hard. Glass shattered on the kitchen floor. Someone hit the wall hard. World War III had broken out in my apartment. It was time to get lost.

I had one leg over the radiator when I felt the hot .45 burning a circle on the back of my neck.

"Just tell me where the damned thing is," said the pudgy man.

"It's not here," I said.

"I know." He nudged me out onto the fire escape. "We'll go get it." I looked behind him and could make out the two cops scattered like rag dolls in the kitchen entrance.

"Who the hell are you?" I said.

"Let's go," he said.

I swung my leg over the radiator and ledge, feeling with my foot for the steel grid of the landing. Even when I found it, it was like stepping into space. Through the one-inch squares below my feet I could see a shiny car in the alley, trashcans, and the gooseneck of a broken back door light. I touched the brick wall to steady myself, then felt the nudge of the .45 in the small of my back.

"Down," he said with a shove.

I stumbled, groping for the stairs, but caught the rail and did not fall. My foot was in the air, reaching for the top step, when something moved in the alley below.

"Hold it," said a voice. "Slattery?" Two flashlight beams froze us.

The man behind me swung the .45 towards the lights below. I spun, snapping my fist around like the knob on the end of a baseball bat. The fist connected with his jaw and *crack!* he was going, going, gone. He flopped backwards, the Army Colt hanging loose from one finger.

I reached for the gun, but his back caught the rail and he began to go over. I grasped his knee. The fabric slid through my arms, until all I held was his boot. He caught then. His knee was bent over the rail and he hung backwards, the gun still stuck on his index finger swinging like a pendulum.

I couldn't pull him in and I didn't want to let him go. I didn't even know who he was, yet, and I had questions.

The entire fire escape screeched as one of the men below pulled down the telescoping ladder and scrambled up.

Who are *you?* I thought. My trick for attracting fish had worked too well. This was getting to be a hell of a party.

I glimpsed a flattened nose as the man reached over. He gripped the dangling man by the collar and began lifting him over with one hand.

"Watch the gun," I said, holding the leg.

"He's cold as a cucumber," said the man. He dropped the man in black on the grid like a big Raggedy Andy. I quickly pulled the .45 off his limp finger and sagged panting into the corner of the fire escape.

A second man came up from below. He had a scar on his face from his nostril across his lips to his chin. "You Slattery?" he asked.

I nodded and moved the gun across my knees to make sure they saw it. "Who's he?" he said.

"Who are you?" I asked.

"Are you boys all right out here?" A familiar head stuck out through the window.

"The guy's out," said the flat-nosed man.

"I—I had to tap that phony cop in there," said Jimmy Stewart, rotating a billy club. "He started coming out of it when I was cuffing him. He's sleeping like a baby, now, though. Are you all right, Chess?"

I looked at the two men, then Stewart. "Don't tell me you want the book?"

"What book? Oh, that. You mean Baby Lowen's book? Naw—"

"This is about Baby Lowen?" asked one man. "The girl who got murdered?" The other man whistled.

"Hitch thought you might need some cavalry," Stewart continued. "This here's Skip and Tom. They're stunt men and mighty handy in a pinch."

Skip and Tom tipped their hats. "This is about Baby Lowen?" Tom repeated. I lowered the gun.

"Tom here was a middleweight contender, weren't you, Tom?"

"A long time ago."

"Thanks," I said, blinking. I grabbed the rail and pulled myself to my feet. It wasn't easy. I asked myself how much of a man's body can be bruised before he dies.

"Did you find out what you wanted to know?" asked Stewart.

"No," I said, "but I mean to."

"Hitch told us not to interfere unless it looked bad," said Stewart. "Actually, he told me to stay out of it, but I got kind of bored."

"Then we heard the gun," said Skip.

"Nobody's shot," I said, "but it's changed my ideas about the cleverness of being bait."

The man in black moaned.

"Jimmy," said Tom, "you better get out of here before you're seen."

"It doesn't bother me," he said.

"No," I said, "he's right. You don't want to get mixed up in this. The papers will have a field day."

"Don't they always?" Stewart shrugged. "If you say so, then." He stuck a long leg out the window and started down the fire escape, scooting down the ladder at the bottom as if deplaning from his combat bomber.

"Let's get this moke inside before he comes out of it," I said. "He's a dangerous son of a bitch."

Skip and Tom each grabbed an arm and carried the man inside. We tied him to a dinette chair with two leather belts and three extension cords, making sure he couldn't move his legs or his arms. His head rolled around, but he didn't regain full consciousness until he was totally bound.

I went into the living room and looked down at the phony cops. One was blinking. His mouth was bloody. I shoved him onto his back and turned on the light in the kitchen.

Yeah. He was one of the guys who had grabbed Baby. And now they had come to grab me.

"So," I said, "what's your name and how come you're running around impersonating a police officer?"

"You better let me go. You're interfering with an officer in the performance—"

"Cut the crap," I said. "The badge is real, but you're not."

Tom came out of the bedroom. "Sleeping Beauty's coming around."

"Right," I said. I put my foot on the phony cop's chest. "Don't go anywhere."

"If they try anything," I said to Skip, "aim for the nuts."

"No problem," he said.

I went back to the bedroom. The man in black was struggling against his bonds.

"Take it easy," I said. I set up my lamp and clicked it on.

He raised his head. I could see through his mask that his eyes were wet. He was weeping. "I thought I could get it and no one would be the wiser."

"Okay, Zorro," I said, "let's take off the mask."

It was tied in the back and it took some picking to get it loose. When I peeled it off his bald noggin, however, I was flabbergasted.

"Jesus," I said. "You?"

"Who is he?" asked Tom.

"Mr. Peepers," I said.

CHAPTER
TWENTY-ONE

It was a lucky punch," said the pharmacist. He clearly wanted a rematch.

"Well, I'll be damned," I said. "What have *you* got to do with this?"

"Who is he?" repeated Tom.

"He runs a drugstore across the street from Leo Ventuno's studio."

"He's a druggist?"

"His daughter said he was some kind of commando or something like that in dubya two."

"Him?"

"He handled the two in the living room like they were the Bobbsey Twins."

"I've lost my edge," said the pharmacist.

"No," I said. "I got lucky."

The pharmacist took several deep breaths. "I could have killed you if I wanted."

I squatted to look him in the face. "I got lucky. What's the story?"

"The bitch!" he said.

"Baby Lowen?"

"Going to be a big star. Doesn't care who she steps on getting there."

Maybe it took the knocking around to make the light bulb go off in my brain. "She worked for you."

He lowered his eyes. Where had I heard she had worked at a lunch counter when she first came to Los Angeles? I hadn't thought anything about it. Lots of girls did that.

"Where was your daughter?" I asked.

"My stepdaughter. Her father died in 1940."

"You adopted her?"

"Velma came with the marriage. My wife is older than I am, and she isn't well."

I was beginning to hear a familiar tune. My wife is sick. A man has needs.

"Velma was still in school when Christina—Baby—worked for us. Baby quit about when Velma decided to quit school. My wife made me give Velma the job. We thought she'd go back to school after a few months."

"All right," I said, "so Baby shows up and you give her a job and one thing leads to another."

"No!"

I put my hand on his knee. "Look, buddy, it's no skin off my nose. She comes on to you—"

"She did come on to me. Once or twice. Or I thought she was. The way she was, well, she came on to everybody. She liked to reel them in and toss them back. I didn't mind. It helped the counter trade."

"So, she made you want her, but she was just teasing. And this made you pretty mad, I guess."

"No!"

"Then what was it? Why'd you kill her?"

He struggled, the chair squeaked against the floor. "I didn't kill her!"

I went down on one knee. A symphony of aches was playing in every part of my body. "Look. I'm thinking about the way she was killed. It would take somebody with some kind of experience to do that. I'm thinking about your war record. I'm thinking that Leo Ventuno was right across the street. He maybe saw something, or Baby told him something he brought back at you. A little blackmail? Sounds logical to me."

"No!"

"And then I'm thinking about the way the cuts on Ventuno's body came from something long and sharp, and, hey, I'm thinking bayonet."

"I didn't kill anybody!"

"Look, the bitch comes on to you. The bitch wants to use you. I can understand how you felt. If you talk about it, maybe the police will understand, too, and then—"

"I'm telling you that isn't the way it happened!" he shouted.

I was suddenly squeamish about how easily I had reverted to homicide dick. Talking about Baby in that way, even to trick her killer into confessing, felt dirty. It had been too easy to be a cop. Tossing me off the force made me see it all different somehow.

"Okay," I said, "tell me what happened."

He had put up a sign: "Lunch Counter Girl, Some Cooking." The first girl burnt out the coffee pot, but Baby Lowen could not only make coffee and whirl up a shake, she could even cook eggs and ham and such when the cook was late.

And guys came back. Some days there wasn't an empty stool in the lunch area. It made him a little suspicious. He watched her in case she was running the whore game on the side, but she seemed to be tempting and not delivering. She came on strong whenever a guy showed up who might have movie connections, but otherwise she was just honing her vocation, as he put it.

"I mean vocation, too," he said. "She had a real calling for this. She could drive a man crazy when she decided to, but be nothing special when she had the switch off. If only she could have done that in a movie . . ."

Baby noticed him watching her and assumed he was interested. She came back to talk to him after the lunch counter closed. She asked him for rides home. He was tempted. Hell, she was young and pouty. She had that strange mixture of virgin and slut that makes men salivate.

He wasn't actually sure why he'd never made a move. Maybe it was because he'd seen her toy with other men. Maybe it was because he'd gotten a bad dose from a woman in Australia during the war. Maybe it was just because she reminded him a little of his stepdaughter.

After a few weeks, however, he began to notice some odd things in the storeroom. A woman came in for some cold cream and the box was nearly empty. Women didn't go for the big jar of Pond's all that often. They usually went for the smaller one.

"Pond's?" I said. I held out my hands. "A jar about that big?"

My surprise seemed to confuse him.

"Yeah. That's it," he said uncertainly. "I asked her if she knew what happened to them.

"She winked and said actresses used a lot of the stuff to wash off their Max Factor and I knew she had taken it. I figured she had stolen about half a dozen jars. I mean, one or two, okay maybe, but six or seven?"

"Pond's jars?" What did it mean?

"Yes," he said, irritated.

"Go on," I said.

He was relieved that she decided to quit. She said the job was interfering with her auditions. But he'd noticed she wore much better clothes all of a sudden, a pearl necklace it made no sense to slop coffee in. He figured she had found a sugar daddy and that was the end of that.

But a week before she was killed, she had shown up again. He was locking up the store and she appeared on the sidewalk. She looked lousy, pale, and red-eyed. She had dark circles under her eyes. She said she needed to talk to him. They went inside and sat at the counter stools.

"I need your help," she said.

"You don't look well," he said.

"I need a doctor."

"Dr. Hester is good, and a lot of people like Dr. Solomon, up on Franklin."

"No," she said. "No. I need a special doctor, somebody who can help me."

The first thing he thought of was junk, but why go through a doctor? There was enough in the back to keep her flying until she was ninety.

"I need," she told him, "somebody who can take care of my problem. I just can't get stuck with a kid. I'd rather be dead."

He was shaken by what she said, more by the collected way she said it, than by what she was saying. Women had come to him before with this problem and he hadn't helped them, even though their lives might be ruined. Their husbands would find out. Their fathers would find out. Their fiancées would find out.

Baby thought her life was going to be ruined because she would be cut out of auditions.

He thought of his daughter again and it outraged him. He felt sorry for Baby, but he was mad she'd asked him. He told her to get lost. She'd made her own bed and she ought to go back to wherever she came from.

He slid off the stool and moved toward the front door. He had already stuck the key in the door lock, when he realized she hadn't followed him.

If he thought she was cold before, he said, he had a lot to learn. The orange light from the sunset colored her pale face an inhuman hue.

"I'll say it's yours," was all she said.

"What?"

"You heard me."

"It's a lie," he said.

"It won't matter."

"There are blood tests," he said.

"They don't always work."

He again thought of his stepdaughter. And his wife. And everything he had worked for since he had married her in 1942. If the woman had been well, he said, he might have thrown Baby through the window.

He thought a moment. "Look, I don't know who does that sort of thing. Would some money help? Maybe I could lend you some money."

"Three hundred," she said.

"I can't give you three hundred!" he said. "Who do you think I am? I just paid the rent. Maybe a hundred. . . ?"

"Two," she said, "or you've got another kid."

"Why do you want to do this to me?" he pleaded. "I've never done anything bad to you."

She cocked her head to one side, but said nothing.

"Get the hell out of here," he finally said. "Say anything you like!"

"*You* could help me," she said.

"Use your own coat hanger," he said.

"You've got stuff back there."

"I don't know anything about that," he said.

"But you know."

"I know the stuff could kill you. That's all I know."

She had stepped toward him and run a finger down his lapel. "Mix it up for me," she had said, "and you'll never hear from me again."

I interrupted his story. "Is there a drug for this? Did you give it to her?"

He stared straight ahead. "You can make it happen. You've got to poison her just enough to kill it, but not enough to kill her." His head dropped. "I thought about it. I thought about it real hard. A little too much. . . . It would be an accident. She had stolen stuff before. I could even make it look like a suicide: Phenobarbital and arsenic."

"But she wasn't poisoned, was she?"

"No. I hated myself for thinking it. I lost control. I reached out with one hand and grabbed her by the throat. With the other hand I opened the door. I threw her out onto the pavement."

"And then?"

"She screamed at me. She was going to make me sorry and this and that."

"And then?"

"And then nothing. She left. I decided to go home and tell my wife what she was going to say, but the chest pains were on her and I couldn't bring myself to do it."

I thought for a moment. "You grabbed Baby by the throat?"

He nodded.

"Did you hit her with your fist?"

"No."

"On the jaw. Here. Did she maybe hit her jaw when she fell down?"

"I don't know," he said. "What difference does it make?"

I was thinking that the diner clerk had said she had a bruise on her jaw at three a.m. the next morning. "If you didn't do anything with her, how come you've tried so hard to get the book?"

"God knows what she wrote in it," he said. "She might have said anything. I was nuts with worry. Any kind of shock could kill Esther. I thought it would be easy. In. Out."

"It turned into a helluva party," grunted Tom.

"Didn't it?" I said. "So you tossed the place and then came back to get it out of me."

"I didn't come in until you caught me. I was watching from across the street. I saw a big man come in the front. I waited until he left. He didn't seem to be carrying anything. You must have come in while I was changing."

I thought of my sofa standing on its end. "This big man. Describe him."

"His hat was pulled low. He was wearing a suit."

"A nice suit?"

He shrugged. Arnie, I thought. "Is that it?" I asked.

He nodded.

"What now?" asked Tom. "Call the police?"

"It'll kill her," the pharmacist said sadly.

"Screw the cops," I said. "Where are they? They should be staking me out. All this going on here and I'm getting tossed around like a dishrag."

"What about him?"

Mr. Peepers, commando. "Listen, buddy," I said. "Forget about the book. You're not mentioned in it at all. Forget about it. Deep six the outfit and go take care of your family. You're too old to relive the glory days."

Tom began loosening the wire around his shins.

"You'll keep my name out of it?"

"If you didn't lie to me, I already forgot your name. I don't know who you are. Get the hell out of here and you'll remain nameless."

CHAPTER
TWENTY-TWO

The phony cops had come to and Skip had set them on the sofa, their arms still handcuffed behind them. The one with the wattle had a knot on his balding head the size of a Faberge egg, and just about as colorful. The other had a black eye. Quite an attractive group we were.

"Let us go," said the one with the wattle, "and we won't press charges."

I reversed a dinette chair and sat opposite them. "Not a good deal. I tell you what? You tell me all you know and maybe I'll develop a kind streak."

"Meaning what?"

"Meaning maybe I won't let Tom and Skip here do the tarantella on your face."

"Look at the badge! We're cops."

"Don't make me laugh. I don't know where you got the uniforms and badges, but you're not cops. I know cops. Even with this nose I know they smell better than you two."

They looked at each other.

"I bet if I call in those badge numbers we'll find out who they're stolen from. That'll get you a few years in San Quentin."

"Don't," said the younger man. "It was just a gag."

"A gag? Maybe you start by telling me what Pete's up to?"

"Pete?"

"Look, I'm already ticked off, here, and—"

"Jess Johnson!" said Tom.

"You're right," said Skip.

"Son of a bitch," muttered the guy with the wattle.

"What are you doing, Johnson?" Tom asked.

Johnson looked like he needed a Bromo.

"You know these mokes?" I asked.

"He used to do stunts for Republic," said Tom. "I don't know the other one."

"Crashed a stagecoach into a set," said Skip. "Killed two extras."

"Served a couple of years for reckless something or other," said Tom.

"It was an accident," said Johnson. "They goated me!"

Now I had a theory why he looked somewhat familiar. Maybe I'd seen him in a Saturday matinee. I watched a lot of bad Westerns when I first got back from the war. They took my mind off things.

"Never mind that," I said. "What's Pete Cohn up to?"

"We don't work for Cohn. Who's Pete Cohn?"

"No? Then what were you doing grabbing Baby Lowen off the Bel Air golf course?"

They looked at each other again.

"It was just a favor," said the younger one.

"Shut up, Butch," said Johnson. "Who's Baby Lowen?"

"What's the matter, Johnson? You want Butch to keep you company on death row?"

"Death row?" said Butch.

"Stick it in your ear," said Johnson.

"Sure. Somebody's got to take the fall, right? Look what nice packages you two make, all wrapped up like Christmas in the uniforms you stole."

"We didn't steal them," said Butch. "My brother—"

"Shut up!" said Johnson. "I'll take you apart like a cheap watch!"

"What was that you were saying about your brother? Don't tell me your brother's a cop?"

Butch darted a glance at Johnson.

"Does he know what you're doing with the uniforms?"

"I'm not going to jail over this," said Butch to his partner, who now needed about a gallon of Bromo. "We paid him. He thinks it's a gag."

"Some gag, killing Baby Lowen!"

"No," said Butch, "we were just supposed to run her out of town. We were supposed to grab her and take her to the train station and send her on the first outbound. That's it!"

"We never saw her after that," grumbled Johnson, shooting an evil look at his partner.

"After what?"

"We picked her up, see, but she was a real wildcat," said Butch. "She was kicking and biting and we had to cuff her. We drove out to behind a factory and started giving her the speech."

"The speech?"

"We were supposed to say we were going to run her in as a hooker. It would be on her record and all. We'd say we could see how good girls was used by these Hollywood types and we felt sorry for her. But we would give her a break if she left town and never came back."

"She bought it?"

"Well, she started to cry and I felt a little bad about it."

"She was real good," said Johnson, "better'n half the broads you see on television."

"So, she was crying," continued Butch, "and she said she was grateful and all and that all she wanted to do was go back home and find her fiancé and ask his forgiveness and so on and so on."

"Then she started to say it would be hard because she had really discovered what a good strong man could do for a woman." Johnson looked humiliated by the thought.

"So we uncuffed her," said Butch.

Johnson shook his head.

I grinned. "And Baby got the drop on you?"

"When she got our pants loose—"

Tom made a face. "You guys were going to do it at the same time? Geez!"

"She got them around our ankles and—"

Tom, Skip, and I laughed out loud. I could see them stumbling and grabbing at their trousers as she blew a kiss at them and ran. Butch and Johnson turned red.

"She ran away, okay?" said Johnson. He tried to stand. I shoved him back on the sofa.

"And you never saw her again?"

"No," said Johnson.

"I swear," said Butch.

I thought for a moment. "Which one of you clipped her on the jaw?"

"We never laid a finger on her," said Butch. "We just grabbed her, that was all."

"She already had a bruise. Near her ear," said Johnson.

"So how did you come to grab her?"

"I took her around the waist from behind—"

"No," I said, "how at the country club? What was she doing there?"

"The boss got a tip earlier in the day that she'd be there," said Butch. "That gave us time to get the uniforms and so on."

"How did he know that?"

"I dunno. He told us to wait in the rough near the eighteenth hole."

"There we were," said Johnson, "and there she was."

"So we grabbed her," said Butch.

"Did she say why she was at the country club?"

They shook their heads.

"Did you see where she was headed?"

"She came out of the parking lot, went around the edge of the green, and then headed across. That's when we rushed her."

I stood and paced a moment. Why was she headed toward Hitchcock's house? What was she thinking? That she would accuse him of fathering her child? She might have been desperate, but she had to know that wouldn't work. Maybe she just thought he would give her money to avoid the annoyance of the accusation. But he had never been anywhere near her, as far as I knew, and by this point, I had no reason not to believe him.

"When she was bawling in the car," said Butch, "she said we'd messed up her chance, or something like that."

"What do you mean?"

"I'm not sure. She said everybody was stopping her when she had a chance to show what she could do. She said we'd messed up her big chance."

"Like she was on her way to an audition?"

Butch shrugged.

"She didn't need an audition," said Johnson. "All that crying and then the, well, like she really wanted—Hell, she caught us good."

"Caught yez with your pants down," said Skip.

"Mr. Funny," said Johnson.

"Hey, it's hard not to laugh at Laurel and Hardy," I said. "Why don't we go see Mr. Cohn and see why he was so interested in getting Baby out of town."

"Huh?" said Butch.

"Cohn doesn't usually send girls out of town. He sucks the life out of them and leaves them to cruise the sailors in Long Beach."

Johnson sneered. "You asshole! What's Pete Cohn got to do with it? We don't work for Cohn."

"Keep humming that tune and I'll make you sorry for it," I said.

"You and what army?" said Johnson.

"We work for Smoky Tex Grady," said Butch.

The hardest part of it to believe was that he was proud of it.

CHAPTER
TWENTY-THREE

I asked Skip and Tom for a favor. If they didn't want to do it they didn't have to, but I already knew they were game boys. Anybody who dives off roofs for a living has got to be. A lot of tourists at the corner of Hollywood and Vine were about to be treated to the spectacle of two handcuffed men being shoved out onto the sidewalk. They would be wearing half of a police uniform, the top half, and be naked from the waist down.

After some scurrying, Jess Johnson and his pal Butch would be cornered by a real policeman. And once the police back at the station found out they weren't really cops, well, the door would close and a couple of the more physical officers would be invited in to impress upon them exactly how unhappy this made the men in blue. It would also be a very bad day for the officer who'd rented them the outfits. He'd be lucky to get my old Pink job.

Meanwhile, I drove back to the place where I had lost my job on the force. Call it a sentimental journey.

The lights were out in front, and when I checked the driveway back to the three-car garage, the house looked dark—all except for the back bedroom window. The garage door had been left open. A huge black Lincoln and a cream-colored Olds convertible dwarfed the red Austin-Healy between them. Good, I thought, my boy's home. He's probably lying up all comfortable in bed, watching *Playhouse 90* over the head of the chippy attached to his crank.

I leaned on the doorbell and waited, standing far back under the portico so that I couldn't be seen from the front windows. It was late enough that the household help would be gone, I hoped, but I didn't want him to send the girl.

When the door opened, I had me a bingo. Smoky Tex barely had time to recognize me and get out half of the word "What?"

My knuckles caught him right across the nose. His red hair snapped up like a whip and he flopped on the floor, sliding on his silk pajamas and bathrobe.

"Hey, Tex, long time no see! Did I drop by too late? Tired from beating up a couple of girls, or haven't you got to it tonight?"

His eyes rolled like a craps master's dice, but he managed to raise himself on one elbow. "My nose!" he whimpered. "You broke my nose again."

"Double or nothing," I said, bringing back my foot.

"No!" he whimpered. "No!" He shimmied backwards on the tiles, slipping and falling back because of the silk.

"Okay," I said. "Only out of my deep respect for you."

"You son of a bitch!" he groaned. The nosebleed was worthy of Cyrano de Bergerac. He stared dumbfounded at his gory hands and the wide stain on his pajamas.

"But also because I'm expecting to hear the truth out of you. You remember the truth? That's the stuff you're always buying, so you can hide it or burn it or whatever it takes to makes it disappear."

"I was supposed to shoot on Monday!"

I glanced around the foyer and into the dark adjoining parlors. Up the stairs I made out some light in the upstairs corridor and heard a loud gunfight from a cowboy show. No, it wasn't *Playhouse 90*. Smoky Tex watch *Playhouse 90?* Hell, that was just another one of those shows with words in it. Who needs words? Next thing you'll want Tex to read or something.

"Oh, gee, Tex, I guess they'll have to work around you."

He moaned and again looked at the blood. He crawled toward a pier mirror by a cowhide wastebasket and stood on his knees. "Look what you did!"

"Shut up and hope your girlie upstairs doesn't interrupt us. How's Jess Johnson?"

"Jess? Where is Jess?" He staggered to his feet. He was tightening his fists.

I wasn't in the mood and pulled my Smith and Wesson. "Let's step in this study here and chat, Mr. Grady."

He glanced up the stairs.

"Real quiet," I added. "I just want some answers."

He backed into the dark. He did it too easily. I figured he had a gun hidden in the desk or on the mantle, probably a genuine simulated cowboy six-shooter. "That's enough," I said.

"Can't we sit? I feel dizzy."

"Get on your knees, then. In the middle of the bear rug. Go on. Down. I'm not going to hurt you unless I have to."

He dropped. Blobs of dark blood from his nose patted onto the bear's head. I waited.

"What happened to Jess?" he sniffed.

"He's not doing too well. He ran into a judo expert."

"Okay," he sighed, "how much do you want?"

"I thought I'd go to the highest bidder," I said.

"If you'll give me a few days, I can make it pretty sweet for you."

"What? You'll give me a nice funeral? You haven't exactly played me square, Smoky or Tex or whoever you are."

"Jess told me he could get the book easy. I told him no rough stuff."

"I'll bet."

"In two days, my agent's supposed to give me a check for ten thousand. It's yours."

"Ten thousand?"

Smoky Tex was encouraged. "Yeah. No hard feelings. You know it wouldn't be anything but trouble for a while. I'd ride it out, but it would maybe slow things down. You know how it goes. The morals clause and all that."

"They wouldn't like to hear about Baby Lowen and Smoky Tex would they?"

"Hey, I'm no worse'n anyone else, partner."

"That's up for debate, partner."

"What did she say in the book?"

"Enough." I glanced up the stairs. Nothing had changed. "Well?"

"It was just a party or two. A little reefer, a few bennies. I wasn't the only one who did her. It was just a fun time."

"I hear kids watch your movies."

"There might be a television deal."

"I doubt it."

Tex shook his head. "All right. Sure. You got me. Ten thousand when I get paid. Ten thousand next month. Whattaya say? That's a lot of scratch."

"Well, like you say, you weren't the only one. That's why I'm thinking auction."

He smiled a desperate smile. "That's exactly my point. Sure, I could be the father. But so could the other two guys at the party in July! Am I right? Do I deserve worse than them? Does she come to them? No, she comes to me!"

"I guess she figured that you have the money."

"She said she'd blab it around unless I helped her get rid of it, got her in my next movie and on the television show. Yeah, right."

"So you punched her."

"I gave her a tap. Yeah. Whattaya expect? I was a little crocked when she got here. It was nothing more than a love tap."

"Don't tell me you loved her?"

"You're a funny guy," he said, wiping his face with his sleeve. I could see from the foyer light he was bluing up nicely.

"I'd have given her more, the bitch, but she got away."

"Yeah?"

"Ran out the door."

"You let a little Tweety Bird like that run away from you?"

He avoided my eyes. "She was saying 'Don't hurt me, don't hurt me!' and she went down on her knees. Then she came up with that purse of hers."

"Ouch," I said, grinning.

"It wasn't funny. It made me puke."

"You know Tex, for a Western hero you sure get beat up a lot."

"Oh shut up," he said.

"So you had Jess and Butch grab her and kill her."

"No! Sure I wanted to teach the bitch a lesson. Hell, who was she to do this to me? But I thought, no, the thing to do was get her out of town, that's all. I thought maybe Jess could take her down to Mexico, maybe sell her to a cathouse. But he said things didn't work that way. They don't need to buy women. He said he knew a way to scare her off."

"And what if that didn't work? Whoo, cowboy, that's it, isn't it? It didn't work. She came back for more and *then* you killed her."

"Slattery, I swear to you I never saw her again."

"But you sent Jess and Butch to get her, right?"

"That doesn't mean I saw her."

"It meant you knew where she was. You knew she was going to the country club."

"I had everybody looking for her. Everybody she might contact."

"Like who?"

"Like everybody I could think of. Leo Ventuno, the poor son of a bitch."

"Small world. I didn't know you knew Leo."

"He introduced me to some girls."

"Baby?"

He nodded.

"Who else?"

"There was Karen and Sylvia and the spitfire, a black-haired Mexican—"

"I met the Mexican when I came into your sorry life," I said. "She was spitting her teeth at the time, wasn't she? In any case, Crap-for-Brains, I meant who else did you call—"

The doorbell rang.

"You expecting anyone?"

Tex shook his head. "I swear," he said.

The doorbell rang again. Whoever it was started pounding. The bushes blocked the view from the study window, but I could see the steady red pulse of a bubble top. Maybe the girl upstairs had called it in.

"Well," I said, "don't keep them waiting. Just remember what's pointed at you."

He stood and walked awkwardly, as if his legs had gone to sleep. He glanced back at me. I smiled. He opened the door.

"Thank God!" he said. "You're—"

"Are you Herman Enoch Grady?"

"Why you know I—"

An arm shoved him back. Sergeant Everson, followed by Detective Dixon and Captain Greene stepped inside. Dixon went for his gun when he saw me. Greene grabbed him before he unholstered it. I raised my hands.

"There you are," said Greene. "Don't tell me you've been using this creep for a punching bag again!"

"There's not much exercise," I said. "He's got a glass nose."

"Officer, the man busts into my house and threatens me—"

"With what he knew about Baby Lowen," I said.

Herman Enoch grew suddenly silent. "I was joking, officer, we were just into a little horseplay, just mixing it up, and—"

"Shut up," said Greene. "We've been talking with Jess Johnson. You know who Jess Johnson is?"

"Sure, officer, Jess was a stunt man in *Arrows Over Tucson*. He sometimes does odd jobs—"

"Like dressing up like a cop?"

"He did what?"

Greene's mouth twisted like he'd just found half of a cockroach in his minestrone. "Jess, and his pal Butch, have been warbling like Ethel Merman, and guess what? They had a lot to say about you."

"They're liars, officer. You can never trust 'em. Too much red-eye, if you know what I mean."

"Ain't that a shame!" said Greene. "They're liable to hurt your career with their scurrilous accusations! They might even put you on death row!"

"Smoky Tex did it?" I asked.

"He had the motive, I figure, and the means."

Grady's mouth fluttered like the flap on a diesel exhaust. The cowboy was beginning to look a might peak-ed, I thought.

"Once you give us that book," said Greene, "like you should have done in the first place—that ought to ice it."

I glanced at Tex, then said to Greene, "Come in here to the parlor. I'll tell you where it's hidden."

"I didn't kill the bitch!" said Grady.

Everson whacked him across the thigh with his billy. "You shut up," he said.

I pulled Greene close to me. "There is no book," I whispered.

"What?! Everybody in town knows—!"

I shrugged and rolled my eyes toward Grady. "I was just getting the bugs to come out from under the rocks. I planted the story."

"Well, Jesus H. Mulligan!" said Greene. "That about—"

"*He* doesn't know it," I whispered.

"Ahhhh," said Greene. "I get you. Listen, I never thought you were a bad cop. I'm sorry about—"

"Forget it."

"When we bring this bastard down, maybe this will get you back on the force."

I didn't know what to say.

"Maybe I'll take a whack at him myself," said Greene.

"Don't bother. It's like kissing your Aunt Rose. Get a confession out of him. Did I mention he knew Leo Ventuno?"

Dixon interrupted. "He wants to get his clothes on. I figured we'd drag him down there in his pajamas."

"There's a lot of blood on them," said Greene. "We don't want to look like we've been beating the stuffing out of him when he confesses."

"Okay." He turned to go.

"Watch it," I said. "He's got guns around you can bet."

"I'll go up and get the clothes," said Dixon.

"He can dress right there in the foyer," said Greene.

"Sure," said Dixon. "You hold him," he said to the sergeant.

"I didn't kill the bitch," said Grady. "Honest."

Greene looked back at him. "You shut up until you tell me something I want to hear." He faced me again and winked. "It sure worked. I should have thought of that. So there was no diary?"

"She had an autograph book," I said, "but it's probably been sold off to some collector or thrown in the trash. Who knows?"

"Did it have anything in it?"

"The landlady said it had a nice inscription from Errol Flynn in it. That's all I know."

"Still, I'd like to have it," said Greene. "It might have been something to use against Tex. He gets a good lawyer and—you know." He yawned. "Did you hear somebody tried to get into Flynn's house again? I was over there until two a.m. last night. This time the burglars tried to drug the dogs, but they sicked up. If you get back on the force, don't become a captain. Every celebrity who hears a bump wants you to look into it personally."

"Tonight's worth staying awake for."

He nodded.

"Listen, why didn't you stake out my apartment?" I asked. "I figured you would."

"How do you know I didn't?"

"A lot of bugs came from under the rocks. Not all this on my face is old."

He squinted. "I see." He leaned forward confidentially. "I got a call."

"A call?"

"That you wanted the surveillance pulled."

"It was probably Tex."

"Tex? I wouldn't do crap for Tex. It was the big man." He pursed his lips and laced his fingers over his belly.

"Hitchcock?"

He winked.

He could have gotten me killed was my first thought. But that also explained Skip, Tom, and Jimmy Stewart.

"Captain!" shouted Dixon from the stairs. "Quick!"

His tone of voice told us all we needed to know. We charged past Sergeant Everson, who was handcuffing Tex to a thick baluster.

"What is it?" said Tex. "What is it?" He jerked against his cuffs.

Dixon waved us on. We crossed the marble-tiled landing and a white carpet deep enough to get lost in. Dixon pointed into the back bedroom. All I saw was a huge round white bed with a peaked canopy. The pillows were tossed and the satin bedspread was rumpled.

The captain stepped through the door and swung his head to the left, "Jesus H. Mulligan!" he said with a whistle. "Is he alive?"

"Does he effing look alive?" said Dixon.

The louvered closet doors were open. Slumped on the dozens of pairs of cowboy boots was a thin man, wearing only a pair of blue silk pajama bottoms. His chest was shiny wet with blood. It had sprayed up on the row of western shirts above him. With his head lolled back at an unnatural angle, he looked like he had two mouths.

"He nearly cut his damned head off!" said Dixon. He spun toward me. So did Greene.

"Hey," I said, "forget me. I never came upstairs."

Sergeant Everson had followed us. He stuck a gun into my spine.

"Hey!" I shouted. "Look at all the blood on him. Look at all the blood on me."

"Put that away, sarge," said Greene. He bent to look at the body. "Who is this moke, and why would Tex want to kill him?"

"Was he sleeping here?" asked Dixon.

"If so," I said, "where was Tex sleeping?"

Greene's eyes met mine. The same notion occurred to us at the same time. I thought Greene actually blushed a bit. "Ick! Not one of these things. Get that pervert up here!" he snapped. Everson rushed down the stairs.

"Couldn't be," I said. "Could it? Baby thought he made her pregnant."

"What are you, some rube from Barstow? Jesus H. Mulligan, Slattery!"

He was right, of course. There were plenty of guys around who, if they got it up, didn't much care how they got it down.

"That's one thing I never pegged Tex for," I said.

"You were too busy hitting him."

I moved toward the body, but had only taken a step when there was a muffled cry and a thump. All of us spun toward the hallway. Both Dixon and Greene pulled their .38s, and we all moved cautiously toward the door.

The noise was from downstairs. There was running, a slammed door.

"Everson!" shouted Greene. "Sergeant!"

When no one answered, we charged for the stairs. I skidded on the landing, nearly going over the rail. Glass shattered somewhere.

At the bottom of the stairs Everson lay like a discarded duffel bag. Greene knelt and touched his shoulder. Everson moaned.

I pointed toward the study. The door was now closed.

"Come out!" shouted Greene. "You're under arrest!"

Crouching, we moved across the foyer and took up positions on each side of the door. "I'll kick," I mouthed.

Greene nodded. I silently counted by lifting fingers.

One. Two. Three!

My heel struck the door and it flew back. Greene spun and dived, and ended up nose to nose with the bear rug. We both fired when the window curtain moved, but our bullets flew harmlessly into the night.

There was no window. Tex had smashed it out.

"Captain!" shouted the patrolman. Simultaneously we heard the cranking of a car engine.

"Out front!" I said.

Greene jerked back the door and we glimpsed Tex in the patrol car. "Stop!" Greene bellowed. "In the name—"

Tex swung up a huge nickel-plated revolver and blasted out the passenger window. A huge chunk of door exploded by Greene's head. He fell back, firing. I tried to shoot past him but a piece of doorframe splintered.

Before I could get a shot, the car roared forward. I jumped over Greene and ran down the driveway.

Tex nearly ran head-on into a bus, but managed to veer off. I held my fire. The people on the bus stood and gawked out the back at the speeding patrol car.

I took three quick steps toward my coupe, then slowed. Okay, Tex had gotten away. It wasn't my problem anymore. The murderer would be caught, and that would be that, and Chess Slattery, former police detective, would have nothing to do with it, thank you.

Greene was in the driveway, splinters of door sticking out of his cheek like porcupine quills. "Did he get away? Where is he?"

I shrugged.

"Damn it," said Greene. He spun on Dixon behind him. "You *never, ever,* leave the keys in the car!"

"I didn't," he said.

"You expect me to lie for you?"

The detective lifted his keys out of his pocket and dangled them with his pinkie extended.

"Damn it," muttered Greene.

"I guess you'll have to blame Everson," I said.

"He hot-wired it," said Greene, plucking one of the door splinters from his face and flipping it away like a cigarette butt.

"I guess you get to be captain by thinking on your feet," I said.

"Shut up! He hot-wired it! It doesn't take a genius." He rushed back inside and picked up the fancy phone.

Everson was sitting on the bottom stairs, holding his head, and groaning. I lifted his chin. His eyes were looking in different directions.

"Headed west," shouted Greene into the mouthpiece. "The passenger window is out. He's armed and dangerous and got nothing to lose. If he so much as blinks, you'd better take him down. Understand? Right!" He hung up.

"Judge, jury, and executioner," I said.

"What's your problem, Slattery? He shot at a cop," said Greene. "*Me!* If he surrenders, fine. If he doesn't, that's even better."

"I know the rules, Captain," I said. "You'd better get Everson an ambulance."

"Dixon," Greene said, "get a doctor for Everson, and a meat wagon for the guy upstairs."

"Let's go take another look," I said. "I think I know the guy."

"Yeah?" said Greene.

"He's one of the lower mole rats at Paramount, a publicity guy."

"He'll make the papers tomorrow."

"Sig Fairfax is his name."

"Sig?" asked Greene. "What kind of name is Sig?"

CHAPTER
TWENTY-FOUR

A bottle of ancient cognac in a crystal decanter sat on Hitchcock's desk. He'd offered, I'd taken. A snifter the size of a duckpin bowling ball. I noticed he wasn't having any.

"But of course," said Hitchcock, leaning back in his study chair, "Tex didn't kill Fairfax."

"Why do you say that?" I asked calmly.

"One can hardly slit a throat as you have described and not be drenched in blood."

"It was what I thought, too, while I drove over here. When my heart stopped playing the Mexican hat dance."

He hmmphed. "Why would Greene accept that you didn't do it because you had no blood on you and then determine that Smoky Tex did? It's absurd."

"Maybe he'd rather hang Tex than me. Of course it was Tex's bedroom, not mine. Greene said maybe Tex had washed up in the shower and then came downstairs to answer my doorbell."

"If you had killed a man and his body still lay in your closet ruining your expensive boots, would you answer the door?"

"I've seen weirder, Mr. Hitchcock."

"And then you would carefully clean yourself up before tackling the task of cleaning up Mr. Fairfax?"

"Well, I'm not disagreeing with you. But there is a possibility it happened that way. Maybe he planned to torch his own house. I remember a case like that. It might have worked this time. On the other one there was a bullet in the burned skull. It was easy to know she hadn't died from the fire."

Hitchcock sniffed. "Did you see a stockpile of gasoline, kerosene, or even a high octane scotch?"

"No, but a fire can be started without them. Maybe he was on his way to the garage when I showed up."

"And it was your impression that Mr. Fairfax had only recently been killed?"

"I'd say within minutes. The blood was still wet. None of it had dried that I could see."

"So, then, you see that it must have happened while you were rousting Smoky Tex downstairs."

I spread my palms. "You can kill a man and his heart keeps pumping for a while. Tex could have done it and Sig went on bleeding. When I hit him, there might have been some blood on his pajamas already, but I didn't notice it because his nose ran a gusher as soon as I hit him."

"*Some* blood?"

Hitchcock's implication was right. I could keep piling up justifications until 1992, but it still didn't fit that our boy Herman Enoch had done it.

"Has Lamb turned up?" I asked.

"Not with the studios nor the hospital. John Ferren has heard nothing."

"You know what I think."

"That he will turn up more under the weather than usual."

I raised my eyebrows and sipped the dark cognac.

"There are no unidentified corpses at present," said Hitchcock. "Other than an elderly woman in Santa Monica. And no John Does in the hospitals."

"He could still turn up, stuffed in a trunk in a junk yard."

"Which reminds me," said Hitchcock, "Sigismund Fairfax's convertible."

"Sigismund?"

"I believe that was his full name."

"Yikes," I said, sipping the fine cognac he had poured for me. I was glad Napoleon hadn't got his hands on this batch. "What about the Olds?"

"You saw it when he hired you."

"Yes."

"And then it was in Grady's driveway."

"I didn't connect them immediately. I was too worked up about going after Tex again."

"But you also mentioned the doorman at the country club had seen such a car in the parking lot."

"Yes. I remembered it when they were carting out Sig. I

might have thought of it before, but didn't make much of it."

"He could have been at the country club for a number of reasons, but I doubt he could have afforded to be a member."

"This is what I figure," I said, taking a breath. I was enjoying the heat of the cognac rising like sweet smoke through my brain. "Baby was going from man to man, attempting to get someone to help her out of the pregnancy."

"Precisely," said Hitchcock.

"If Tex and Sid were, well—"

"Indeed."

"And Tex had these parties, as he called them."

"You described a large bed," said Hitchcock.

"Indeed," I found myself saying, despite myself. I blamed the cognac. A few more good swallows and I'd be speaking French. "So Sig was probably one of the partygoers."

"Think of the combinations," said Hitchcock. "It's a mathematical profusion."

"So she may have tried the you're-the-father routine on Sig."

"We can assume so."

I shook my head. "The thing that gets me, though, is why he brought her to the country club. Why would she be coming to you?" I lifted the snifter and tried to make what I was about to say as non-threatening as possible. "I think you know what people would normally think."

It didn't matter, the way I had tried for casualness. His eyes widened. His lips pursed and rolled. The heat from his stare came at me like I had opened a blast furnace.

"Look," I said, swallowing, "I mean I can keep a secret, sir."

"It is obvious why Fairfax brought her here," he said. His voice rose. *"If* you eliminate the *absurd* possibility that *I* would have had a dalliance with her."

"Yes, sir," I said.

He waited.

I shrugged. "I'm sorry," I said. "It's not a fragrant world."

"While it would not be difficult to find out where I live—there are maps of the stars' homes sold on dozens of street corners—it is simpler to recall that Mr. Fairfax had actually been to this house several times, not as a guest, but to deliver things from the studio."

"So he brought Baby to blackmail you?"

"Non sequitur," said Hitchcock. "It doesn't follow."

"Why not?"

"Because he did not pursue blackmail himself after Miss Lowen was murdered."

"I'll buy it. It would be an even better scheme after she turned up dead. No one would want that hanging around his neck."

"Exactly."

"Why then?"

"You are overlooking the simplest and most obvious thing."

"He brought her to be picked up by the phony cops."

"He was," said Hitchcock, "a finger man." He took pleasure in the expression.

"Okay." That made sense to me. Baby went to Sig and threatened a paternity case, or even to blab all about Tex's private parties. Sig calls Tex. Tex tries to think of a private place to kidnap Baby. Sig says he can get her onto the golf course around dark. He sends his flunkies, since she would recognize him. Sig manufactures a reason for Baby to approach the back of Alfred Hitchcock's house.

Baby wouldn't be able to resist that. Perhaps he told her something insane. That Kim Novak was a disaster and Hitchcock was going to fire her and take a chance on an unknown. The biggest lies travel the furthest in Hollywood, and Fairfax certainly knew that. Or perhaps he told her something more routine. Maybe he told her that Hitchcock wanted a private "interview" with her. Baby would have been game for that, in hopes it would lead to a job. She had made that mistake enough times.

"But why," I asked, "did someone send her ear to you? According to Johnson, she got away from them."

"They could have found her later and Smoky Tex carved her up. Or even Smoky Tex and his minions. We know Tex was a strange gamester."

"I don't know," I said skeptically. "What is the connection to you? Other than that Sig brought her here?"

Hitchcock seemed amused. "I am caught in a skein rather like several of my main characters. A man who knew too much."

"But doesn't know what he knows."

"Which reminds me," he said. "When you confronted the gangster, Pete Cohn—"

"And got my face tenderized for my trouble."

"—you saw the Oldsmobile."

"Sig's car! You're right. It was parked outside the Knight Klub." It may have registered with me at the time in a vague way, but I didn't think much of it. Then, it wouldn't have meant much to me that Sig Fairfax was in the club. I didn't have much time before I was being pounded.

"And they told you that a Theodore West was a member."

"Sure," I said. "But so what? Tex and Sig were buying Pete Cohn's booze. Guys with their—uh—wide-ranging interests would naturally find Cohn at some point. They say on the street that if your taste runs to one-legged, wall-eyed, dwarf belly dancers, Pete Cohn will get you one. For a price."

"And what did Cohn say to you?" asked Hitchcock. "He said he tried to help her out."

"That's what he always says. He's very helpful to orphans who can learn the trade."

"But could he have meant that he had intended to help her out of her predicament?"

I whistled. "A coat hanger job?"

He hmmphed. "Wouldn't it be completely logical that Mr. Cohn would know immediately which doctor—or pseudo-doctor—would be amenable to that sort of operation? It would be a requirement for his profession."

I thought out loud. "Operation goes wrong. The evidence—Baby's body—needs to be made unrecognizable as a coat hanger job."

"It's a theory," said Hitchcock. "I have taken the liberty of having Peggy make discreet inquiries. The name of Dr. Josiah Crestmont surfaced."

"Where have I heard—?" I snapped my fingers. "He was at the country club the evening Baby was snatched!"

"Perhaps Mr. Fairfax had set up an appointment with him."

"They weren't seen together."

Hitchcock smiled. "It's an attractive theory, don't you think?"

I stood and walked to the window. "It's more than attractive. It fits like a glove—" Hitchcock's tone of voice nagged at me, however. I looked back at him. "But you don't buy it, do you? Who murdered the rest of them? Did the doctor murder Baby, Leo, and Sig?"

"Of course not," said Hitchcock.

"There were different murderers?"

"Oh no," said Hitchcock. "We shall catch him tomorrow evening."

"What?"

"I will require your services, as I am not of the sort to handle this personally."

"I don't understand. What are you saying?"

"Tomorrow we shall capture the murderer and hand him over to the police. I'll expect you to arrive—let's see—I believe mid-afternoon should be early enough. Pat and Alma should be leaving for our ranch about four. Do not, however, park your car anywhere in the neighborhood. Perhaps you should take a cab to a nearby corner and walk over. It might be safe to park at the country club. It would spoil it all if you were seen."

"Safe? What do you mean 'safe'?"

"Yes, and come prepared, young Lochinvar, to do battle. I am depending on you."

"Whoa, whoa, whoa. I don't feel so young. I've been beaten, kicked, threatened, et cetera, et cetera. I think I deserve an explanation."

"It should be clear to you who is coming by now, but if you are afraid to deal with him—"

"With who?"

"With *whom*," said Hitchcock. "You are very modest to pretend you don't know, but if it bores you too much, please let me know so I can prepare alternate assistance."

"Don't you think it's about time to share your thoughts on this?"

"And spoil the surprise? Tut tut."

"I thought you said I already knew."

He watched me for a moment, like a principal waiting for an explanation of why I'd flipped up a girl's dress. "Errol Flynn," he said.

"Are you nuts? Errol Flynn did it? Robin Hood?"

"I meant that you should consider Errol Flynn. That should make things clearer. But, even if that does not, I will require your services tomorrow. Unless you want to recommend someone."

I stood. "Oh, I'll be here, buddy, just to see what rabbit you want to pull from your hat. Maybe the rabbit will bite you, huh? But wrong or right, you have my pay ready. I've taken enough of this either way."

Hitchcock smiled. "You won't be disappointed. It will be one of my best endings. After all, it will be real."

"Let's just hope," I said, "we're not the ones getting ended."

"Rest up," said Hitchcock, yawning. "We may have a long night. Unfortunately, I will be shooting all day. We must give the appearance of a perfectly ordinary day."

"How is the picture going?" I asked, pausing at the study door.

The great man was asleep in his chair, probably dreaming of murders.

CHAPTER
TWENTY-FIVE

My apartment was still a wreck. I dropped the mattress on the floor and fell on it in my clothes. The sleep was sweet, even with the humid air blowing through the space left by the windowpane Mr. Peebles had removed.

I woke, damp and sore from head to toe. It had been a rough week. I thought I ought to straighten the place up, but I couldn't see the point. It was nearly ten. I thought my watch had stopped. I decided a warm bath might take some of the kinks out and soaked in what passed for luxury for about thirty minutes.

When I stepped out of the bathroom with only a towel around my waist, a pale Freddy Mancik sat on the sofa with Arnie. Pete Cohn stood by my front window smoking.

"What is this?" I said. "They made my apartment a bus stop?"

"You had quite a party here last night," said Cohn, gesturing toward an overturned end table.

"Well, I'm sure your club does better."

"It's like a graveyard," said Cohn.

"What's the matter? Decency become a fad? Just when you think Hollywood's improving?"

"Mr. Funny!" said Arnie.

"The book," said Freddy timidly.

"The damn thing—" said Cohn sputtering. "All that stuff about what might be in it. It gives people the willies. They're afraid there'll be a raid or something."

"Nobody knows what's really in the book," I said.

"But they think they do," said Cohn. "They won't even return my calls."

"They," I assumed, were the big shots on his list of the reliably bribed.

"It'll blow over," I said.

"It's killing me," said Cohn.

"The news has barely gotten out," I said.

"Mr. Cohn wants the book," said Freddy.

"A whole lot," said Arnie.

"Well, you know," I said, "I don't much enjoy people tearing up my place, Pete. You sent that big lug to tear the place up—"

"Who says?" said Cohn.

"Who else would stand my sofa on its end?"

"Mr. Cohn's got a right to protect his interests," said Arnie. "Just say the word, Mr. Cohn, and I'll make him spill his guts."

"Watch out or I'll pull off my towel and traumatize you to death."

Arnie stood. Cohn put a hand on his sleeve. "Look, Slattery, I don't want trouble. And you don't want the trouble I can give. I'll even pay you for the book."

"Pay me?"

"Why not?"

"How much?"

"A grand."

"That seems a little, well, meager, Pete."

"He's Mr. Cohn to you," said Arnie.

"Okay," said Cohn, "a grand and a half. That's all it's worth to me."

"That's hard to believe," I said.

"It's a nuisance."

"Oh, no. It's an investment for you. What's in there is a nuisance for you. Maybe. It's a career breaker for the others in there. They'll pay me more than a measly couple of grand for it."

Freddy cleared his throat. "Maybe it would be a good idea if you did take it, Chess. I mean, what's it to you, huh?"

"Freddy, Freddy, Freddy," I said. "If you had that thing, you'd take the two thou and print the junk anyway. What are you worried about? If you get a pair of cement overshoes, you'll look just like an Oscar, a special Oscar for journalistic integrity. You'll be a legend in this burg. A dead legend, but, hey, you got to make a few sacrifices to get ahead."

"Look, lip," said Cohn, "there's no reason anybody gets hurt. That's why I want it." He came towards me. "I did the girl a favor. She was in trouble. Girls do get in trouble, right?"

"I believe you often help them get into trouble."

"They don't need me, believe me. They do fine on their own. It's just they can do better with the right management."

"You get a better class of coat hanger that way."

Cohn eyed me. I felt a chill. Cement hardening between my toes.

"You think I'm cheap," he said. "Like that's my main line of business."

"Cohn," I said, "I know you're into more manure than I know of, and probably more than I can imagine. If the book screws you up, you know, it's probably the best thing Baby Lowen left this city."

"Let me beat it out of him," said Arnie.

"Chess," begged Freddy.

"No," said Cohn. "You don't mash small potatoes. Chess here is no rube. The book's safe somewhere, isn't it? Something happens to you it's printed all over America." He dropped his cigarette on my linoleum and ground it out.

"Hell," he said, "I don't even know what's in it. There's the slut, showing Errol Flynn's autograph to everybody. Didn't she have Fonda's, too? I don't know. But so what? Leo was telling her about a party she was going to help out at. She's writing down the address. He told her not to write things like that down and she says it helps her remember. Like she couldn't remember!"

"A lot of your girls have memory lapses. Especially when they get to court. They can't remember getting beat up. They can't remember the orgies. They're like that Mexican girl Smoky Tex was pounding. They forget everything."

Cohn grinned. "I can't help that. It must be the junk. Some of these girls get into junk, you know. It's kind of sad."

I was still wearing just a towel, but I wanted to pound him into a grease stain. The presence of Arnie made this an unwise ambition. Somehow I had to get out of this situation.

"Look," I said, "what if I clear everything with you?"

"Meaning?"

"I'll keep you out of it. Where there's some money to pick up, I'll cut you in for ten percent."

"I don't get it."

"It's like this," I said. "I find something juicy in the book about Francis X. Bushman. I check with you to see if it's all right to jack him around. You say yes. I approach him. He pays, you get ten percent. He doesn't, some anonymous guys warn him. That way, I'm not my own muscle."

Cohn thought. "Twenty."

"Fifteen."

Cohn laughed. He looked back at Arnie. "They all sell out eventually, don't they?"

"I'll keep the book, though."

"You freelance anything and you know what'll happen."

"It's a deal." I extended my hand.

He looked at it. "It's wet," he said. "You know what'll happen." He flicked his head to indicate the door.

Arnie stood and shoved a thick finger into my chest. "What'll happen, I'll make sure it happens."

"Bug off," I said.

Freddy raised himself off the sofa and rolled an eye at me. Cohn, who was already in the open door, said to him, "I got an appointment. This nice, clean man will give you a ride. You have a lot in common."

He was getting a lot of pleasure out of the idea that I was now one of his stooges. I imagined him whistling down the stairs.

"Whew!" said Freddy. "They said they were going to beat the book outta me! They thought I just made it up that you had it!"

"It was in your column, Freddy."

"They thought it was just a trick."

"Freddy," I said, "why don't you just get going? I just cleaned up and I'd like to stay that way."

"Hey, I was thinking, suppose we pretend like I got some of the stuff out of the book from another source. It'd be tricky, but if I had the book we could work it so—"

"Freddy, get the hell out of here."

"How'll I get back to the paper?"

"Walk," I said.

"How about cab fare?"

"Beat it."

He grabbed my upper arm. I glared at him. He pulled away.

"Look," he said, "at least tell me what's going on with Hitchcock."

"Nothing's going on with Hitchcock."

"Don't kid a kidder. He's sending his wife away. Sounds like a trip to Reno's in the offing."

"Jesus, Freddy, will you ever quit? Hitchcock getting divorced?"

"Hey, dump his old broad for Kim Novak? Who wouldn't?"

"Where are you getting this crap?"

"I talked to him myself."

"What?"

"The word gets around that she's going up to Frisco while he's staying here alone. So I called and asked."

"If he's getting divorced?"

"No, if it was true. He's never returned a phone call by me. Ever." He shoved the *Herald* toward me. I scanned down his column.

M. of S. in Seclusion

Word on the street: Big Al, the M. of S., is said to be so angry about the behavior of the lovely, but strong-willed Kim that he intends to spend the weekend alone at his house reworking *From Among the Dead.*

The M. of S. denies he is angry with the lovely, but strong-willed Kim. He admits to being upset over the recent disappearance of artist friend Walter Lamb and the murder of Paramount publicity hound Sig Fairfax by Smoky Tex Grady.

All the M. of S. will admit is wanting to be alone for a few days. Yet, rumors persist. Egos on the set? "The whole movie is threatened!" says a technician in the know. A sound stage romance? And who is tangling with who?

"He wants to be alone," I said. "Like Garbo. Leave him alone."

"Oh, come on. You want me to pay you, too?"

"Get out of here, Freddy."

"Won't you let me see the book?"

I lost control, dropped my towel, and grabbed him by the collar.

Freddy bounced down the stairs quite nicely.

CHAPTER
TWENTY-SIX

I decided that strolling down the golf course in normal clothes would be like hanging a sandwich board over my shoulders, so I took a cab to the end of Bellagio Road and walked back to Hitchcock's house. No one had parked on the street and other than a Japanese gardener two houses up, no one saw me. No one that I saw.

Pat Hitchcock answered the door. At first I didn't recognize her as Hitchcock's daughter. I didn't own a television. I later heard she made frequent appearances on her father's television show, more than any other actor, usually playing a maid or some other secondary character. She was dressed in a gray suit and wore one of those tiny, what's-the-point women's hats. It's not big enough to keep the rain off, or keep your head warm, and it doesn't show off diamonds like a tiara. What's the point?

"Come in," she said, glancing furtively behind me. "Father told us part of what he's up to. Why don't you tell us the rest?"

There were several suitcases on the floor. Alma came out of the parlor with two pair of white gloves, evidently trying to come to some decision. She put them down on the biggest valise. "Yes, please," she said, "do tell us what scheme Hitch is unfolding now."

"Does he often unfold schemes?"

"Sometime you'll have to ask him about the blue dinner. I'd tell you myself but there's no time for that now. Come into the parlor."

"I don't know what I can tell you," I said, following her.

"Wait," she said, rushing ahead to close the curtains. I paused by the door. I had only just come in, for crying out loud.

"He's sworn you to secrecy!" said Pat.

"No, I'm afraid not. He hasn't told me anything much."

"Out of the blue, two days ago," said Alma, "Hitch jumps up out of bed. It was rather like when he discovers some idea for a problem in a script. But this time, he neither rushes for a notebook nor shares this brainstorm of his with me."

"He does this often?"

"I sometimes believe he thinks best in his sleep."

"Then what?" I asked.

"He told me that I would be taking a trip to the ranch, that everyone must know about it, and that he would be staying here alone."

I thought of the newspapers. "Well, I guess anyone who wants to know it, knows it."

"But he wouldn't tell me what it is about, Mr. Slattery."

"He told me very little. Just that I should be here."

"But it isn't like him."

"Mother has worked closely with father from the beginning," said Pat.

"Where are our manners?" said Alma abruptly. "Tea, Mr. Slattery. Coffee? We have a lovely almond cake. Pat, why don't you bring Mr. Slattery a piece."

"No, Mrs. Hitchcock, I—"

"And coffee. Bring him coffee. I could tell you aren't much of a tea drinker from the last few times."

"Really, I don't want to be any trouble," I said.

Pat, taking the hint, was already gone.

"Now, then, Mr. Slattery, I want to know."

"I wish I knew."

"There is only one reason he wants me away."

"And that is?"

"Danger. He expects some danger. That is why you are here, aren't you, Mr. Slattery?"

"You can call me Chess."

"Mr. Slattery," she warned me.

"Really. He said he needed me here. That no one outside of you two are to know I am here. I think maybe he wants to ask me something he can use in the movie."

She waved a hand. "You're a very poor liar! In truth, he is expecting to lure that cowboy here, isn't he?"

"Cowboy?"

"Poky Tex Grady."

"Smoky Tex Grady."

"That's him. The one on the lam."

I had never heard 'on the lam' in a British accent. "To tell you the truth, Mrs. Hitchcock, I don't know who the honored guest is to be. I think he wants me here merely as a witness to what is said."

"And I won't do for that?"

"I believe he doesn't want the witness to be known to the guest."

She turned. For a moment I actually believed she was buying it. "Very well," she said. "If you want to create a huge tissue of lies rather than tell me the truth, I won't continue."

She stood up. I decided not to say that I wasn't lying.

"But I swear to you, Mr. Slattery, if harm comes to Alfred Hitchcock, you should beware of me!"

She marched out of the room as Pat came in. Pat set the tray down in front of me and watched her mother march up the stairs. She then looked at me.

"I don't know anything," I said.

"Father is directing again," she said almost to herself. "And we are all his cattle." She tugged at the hem of her suit jacket. "Excuse me, Mr. Slattery, will you?"

"Sure," I said. "Just act like I'm not even here."

"That's how it's supposed to be," she said.

Three o'clock passed into four. Four ticked away until four-thirty, when the shiny limousine pulled into the front driveway. I ducked out of sight into a corner of the parlor. I heard the driver carry out the bags, the trunk closing, and such. After they were all loaded up I heard Alma say something about forgetting the teakettle. She came into the parlor and found me.

"Mark what I said, Mr. Slattery," she whispered. "My husband is not to be harmed!"

"He won't be." She stared at me. "I swear to you. Scout's honor. Whatever you like."

"You look nothing like a Scout," she said, spinning on her heels, "but you had better rise to the occasion!"

After she locked the front door and the limo pulled away the house was unearthly silent. Every move I made seemed to echo. I thought of Sig Fairfax, his throat slit while I confronted Tex downstairs. I took the chair in the deepest corner so that no one could get behind me. I loaded all the chambers of my Smith and Wesson, as well as my .18 ankle piece. I picked up a newspaper but it rustled so loud I exchanged it for a copy of the novel *Lydia Bailey* by Kenneth Roberts. It was something about ships, but I couldn't keep my mind on it.

I kept running the whole business through my mind like an old song. What sort of person was capable of doing that to Baby? Not to mention to that slug Ventuno. I assumed the killer would have split open Sig Fairfax as well, if he hadn't been interrupted. I thought of the pieces cut from Baby and packed in her stolen Pond's jars. Had Sig received one? No one had mentioned it. I thought about calling Greene, but didn't know if I could ask about the jars without revealing that Hitchcock had gotten one. Besides, if someone telephoned to test if the house was empty, the line would be busy.

I think the reason I didn't see what was right in front of

me was that I was still hung up on the pharmacist, Mr. Peebles gone commando. He knew how to get into a house without being seen or heard. He knew how to kill.

Means and opportunity usually speak louder to a homicide cop than motive. Some people kill for a nickel. Others wouldn't kill for a trainload of pure platinum. But the killer always has to have the means and the opportunity. It would take a lot of confidence to enter a house in which two men are downstairs in order to slit the throat of a man upstairs.

The balding pharmacist had the opportunity—and the means. Yet his story convinced me. It fit. What didn't?

I also was frustrated. Some movie director's going to trap the killer. Who does he think he is? This master of suspense stuff was just Hollywood hooey. Mysteries are mostly good for a laugh, and not much of one at that. Hell, I was sure Big Al was going to make a jackass of himself with this one, but I was also afraid I'd end up wearing the ears.

The shadows were pretty long and I was beginning to suspect I'd have to wait in the dark. The phone rang. It continued to ring ten times, twelve, up to twenty at least. When it stopped, I checked my guns again and listened very carefully. I never knew how many sounds a mansion makes as it cools and settles in for the evening.

Ten minutes later the phone rang again. And again. And again. What if it was Hitchcock calling me to change plans? I couldn't risk it. I let it go on for about the same number of rings as before. That convinced me it was the same caller.

I waited.

A car pulled into the driveway. I heard a muffled exchange of words. The car door slammed and a key ground

into the lock. I drew my gun and half concealed myself behind a chair. When the foyer light went on, Alfred Hitchcock
closed his front door.

I stood. "Mr. Hitchcock," I said.

"Quiet," he whispered, "and remain low."

"The curtains are all drawn in here."

"We must wait in my office," he said.

"For what?"

"'For whom,'" he said. "The approach will be from the
rear."

I spread my hands. "And we know this because—?"

"Because it was easy for him before."

"Before? For *whom?*"

He smiled. "You're the detective."

And you're a pompous ass, I wanted to say. If he'd been a
cop, I would have.

But it wasn't what I was really feeling. What I was really
feeling was bafflement and that's what made me mad. I just
wasn't getting it. It was like one of those puzzles in a kid's
book. I was staring and staring, but I couldn't find that last
face hidden in the clouds.

Did I want him to be wrong? No. I had seen two of the
bodies in person. The first victim, Baby, I had seen only in
pictures, but that, oddly enough, was worse. The calendar
nudie. The portfolio nudie. The split torso. The featureless
face.

I could put my ego aside to see this monster fried.
Easily.

Hitchcock stopped outside his study and leaned close to
me. "You will feel your way along the wall to the right and

take up a position in the wingback chair I have placed in the corner. You are not visible from the patio there. After I turn on the light you are not to come out of the corner. I will sit at my desk and work by the light of the lamp."

"What? No cardboard cutout of your profile to project on the window shade. Hey, I know, we could put it on a turntable and it would look like you're dancing."

Hitchcock tilted back his head. It wasn't funny.

I cleared my throat. "Seriously, Mr. Hitchcock, you'd be quite a target through the French doors." I made a gun with my hand. "Pow!"

"I will draw the sheers to obscure his vision somewhat, as that is what I normally do. It is too easy to imagine curiosity seekers watching from the dark. However, the killer is not interested in killing me that way. He wants me to die as the others have died. Suffering."

"So this isn't just gathering the suspects or bearding the lion or something like that. You were serious when you said bait. And Alma was right when she suspected you were getting her out of the house to protect her."

"I couldn't allow anything to endanger her."

"And you're sure the guy won't just shoot?"

"He hasn't shot anyone yet. He probably doesn't even carry a gun. He tries to catch his victims alone. Up until tonight there was always someone else with me: the maid, the cook, Alma. This is obviously personal with him, a crime of passion. Like Mr. Ottermole, he wants to feel his victims suffer and die."

Mr. who? A crime of passion. Somebody who slept with Sig and Baby? And Leo? And Hitch—? That was too weird to contemplate. "I don't get it," I confessed. "Maybe we should talk this over. Maybe you've got it wrong."

"'The game's afoot.'"

"Pardon me, but neither me nor you is Sherlock Holmes."

"Actually, that is a quotation from Shakespeare. Henry the Fifth says it. Prepare for battle."

I sighed. "Okay, so I hide in the corner chair. How long is this going to take?"

"Precisely," said Hitchcock. "A washroom is in there. It is windowless, so you may use the light."

I supposed I wouldn't be getting any of the good cognac tonight.

When I came out he had gone to the kitchen and was holding a cold roast beef sandwich on a long hunk of French bread. "Are you ready?" he asked.

"I don't suppose any of that's for me?"

"Hunger will keep you on edge," he said, pushing open the study door.

I shook my head and stepped into the dark. I extended my arm to the wall and felt the edge of one of the Moroccan rugs under my feet. I bumped into the chair, turned, and sat. "I'm in," I said in a low voice.

He came in as if he were an ordinary Alfred Hitchcock on his way to do some late work. He pulled the chain on the desk lamp, set down his sandwich, and opened a notebook. He glanced out through the dark French doors and then pulled the sheers. He sat and took a big bite of his sandwich.

I stretched out my legs and crossed my arms on my chest. I could smell the strong English mustard from his sandwich. He chewed slowly, as if very aware of my watching. A string of tomato skin briefly hung from his lip. He sucked it in.

"You might turn to your right," he said quietly.

I did. An identical sandwich to his sat on the bookshelf beside me.

"I hope you like it rare," he said.

"It'll do," I said, grabbing the sandwich like it was a brother that went to sea ten years ago. I didn't care that the mustard incinerated the linings of my nose.

I ate slowly. For all I knew I'd be in the chair all night.

Hitchcock thought, scribbled, thought some more.

"Working on *Among the Dead?*" I asked.

"No," he said without looking up. "Anyway, my current film is *Vertigo.*"

"How is that going?"

He gave me a sharp look, then lowered his head. "It is going very well. Henry is always reliable. One of the jurors looked silly at times, but nothing was ruined. And they've worked around the ceiling with much less trouble than they imagined."

I cocked my eye in bewilderment.

Hitchcock didn't lift his head. He was still acting the director hard at work, alone in his office, but I saw lift in his posture. He wanted to explain this. Making movies, that was his life.

"I told Henry Bumstead I wanted a ceiling. He wasn't sure Bob Burks would like it. The camera crew likes to have open fly space. But it all worked out. The audience will be certain it is a location shot. If they give it any thought at all. I suppose I don't want them to give it any thought."

I said "I see," but I didn't. I sat for a few more minutes. "So, Henry Bumstead's a reliable guy?"

Hitchcock nodded. "He is, but I was earlier referring to Henry Jones."

That was an actor, I remembered from somewhere. I couldn't picture him. I nodded. I looked to see what books were within reach. Nothing interested me.

"So what are you working on?"

"I'm not working on anything with these interruptions."

"Sorry."

He exhaled. He kept his head down as if scrutinizing his work, but stopped writing. "Many years ago Otis Guernsey, a journalist of my acquaintance, passed along a story he had heard during the war. It seems an intelligence agency created a master spy in name only and circulated information about him so that the Nazis would come to believe he was real. What if an agency such as the CIA did something similar? What if an ordinary man, not a spy, were to be mistaken for the master spy and the KGB were to set out to kill him?"

"He'd have trouble."

"Indeed. Especially if the CIA couldn't afford to let him off the hook."

"Sounds good," I said.

He lifted his eyes slightly. "What's wrong with it?"

"Nothing," I said.

"You sound unenthusiastic."

"I'm just tired," I said. "It has nothing to do with the story."

"It will be good," he said.

"Spy things—I don't know," I said.

"You will like this one," he said.

"I'm sure I will," I said.

He hmmphed. I supposed he thought I was an idiot, but later I came to understand he was like a child in the middle of his favorite game. He would get so excited about the process of what he was doing that he couldn't understand the slightest lack of interest by anybody else.

"Maybe I'll take a nap," I said.

"Please do," he said.

I had barely closed my eyes when there was a rattle on the patio. I pulled my Smith and Wesson.

"Stay there," said Hitchcock.

I felt the blood pulsing in my neck. Then we heard the faint meow.

"A stray," said Hitchcock.

I holstered my gun. "You're sure he'll be here?"

"If not, I shall have to think again."

"Are you going to tell me who you think?"

His lips curled with amusement. "You still don't know? That will keep you alert."

Defiantly, I straightened out my legs, popped my hat over my eyes, and crossed my arms. I heard him chuckle, still manipulating his audience, and dozed off.

The doorbell shot me to my feet, my hat flying back.

Hitchcock looked toward his patio and muttered to himself. "Sit still," he said.

"What if it's the killer?" I asked.

"He won't ring the bell." He quickly left the room. I hesitated for a moment, thought I couldn't take the chance, and followed him. When I reached the foyer, he was unlocking the door.

"Wait," I said, holding my revolver out in front of me, but the door swung back.

Silhouetted against the distance streetlight was a woman, a very shapely woman. She stepped forward catching the light. Her hair glinted and I recognized her.

"Kim Novak?"

Hitchcock looked back at me. "Of course it's Miss Novak. I told you to stay put. She's no murderer."

"Murderer?" asked Novak. Her eyes widened at the sight of my gun. I lowered it. Hitchcock grabbed her elbow and startled her by pulling her into the foyer.

"Why are you here?" demanded Hitchcock.

"I'm—I'm sorry," she said, glancing at me. "It's just I can't sleep thinking about the next—"

"You're not to report to the set until the thirtieth," he said.

"Well, that's it," she said. "The wait has thrown me off. It's got me a bit worried about the bell tower scene."

"We'll deal with that when we get to it, my dear." He tried to rustle her out of the door, but she refused to be moved.

"I really didn't mean to interrupt anything, Hitch," she said. "But if I could just have a moment. I really appreciate the freedom you give me, I do, but—"

"You're an actress, my dear. I expect you to act, but if you stay, you may ruin something very important."

"I'd be willing to wait. Do I know you?" she asked me. "Weren't you in the band in *The Eddy Duchin Story?*"

She moved toward me with her hand extended. The memory of the way she had danced toward William Holden in *Picnic*, slapping her hands together, shivered through me.

I somehow managed to shake my head no, but no words were coming out.

Hitchcock took her elbow and spun her before her hand met mine. "You *must* go, my dear."

"It's just I want to do my best, Hitch. I know you've got very specific ideas of what you want and I wanted to ask—"

It wasn't loud, the thump I heard behind me at that moment, and it wasn't a stray cat. I raised my gun and turned toward the study.

"Dear God!" said Hitchcock. He looked around, decided against shoving her out the front door, then covered her mouth with his hand and guided her firmly towards the windowless bathroom.

"Lock the door," he whispered. "And, for God's sake, don't come out until I tell you."

Glass shattered, then, and there was no attempt by the intruder to be quiet. He had broken through the French doors. The light clicked off in the study.

Novak gave us a curious look and I momentarily felt weak in the legs. He could kill her, too.

She locked herself in. I flattened myself against the wall next to the office door. The image of a farmhouse in France in 1944 flashed into my mind. I was carrying a rifle and I didn't know what was on the other side of the wall then, either.

With Novak stowed, Hitchcock straightened himself and glanced to see if I was ready. I licked my lips and nodded.

"Hello?" said Hitchcock. "Is that you, Alma? I thought you went to the ranch?"

There was a sweat-trickling silence for a moment. Then a

loud thump, as if the man had lifted the desk a few inches and dropped it.

He was waiting in the dark, trying to draw Hitchcock in.

I signaled maybe I could go out the front door and around the building. Hitchcock touched his watch. He was right. There wasn't enough time. The killer might come out at any second.

Hitchcock reached into his jacket pocket and pulled out a long pair of scissors.

The desk thumped again.

"Alma," he said, "I'm getting a whiskey and going to bed. Good night, dear."

He then made walking motions down the foyer. In a few seconds, I heard someone approach the study door. There was a sweaty smell, something unpleasant I didn't recognize.

Hitchcock backed into the brass umbrella stand, rattling it, and the killer flung open the door.

He was a big man, a very big man, in overalls. The long knife he raised over his head struck the doorframe.

"You ruined my Baby!" he growled.

"I certainly did not," said Hitchcock.

"Drop the knife!" I shouted.

Startled, he turned toward me. A second of surprise turned to madness as he decided that I was just another one in the herd that had to be thinned. His eyes momentarily froze me they were so fevered. The knife flashed downward.

I got off a shot as the knife missed me, but somehow the blade clicked into the gap between the cylinder and the barrel. He pulled back his knife. I pulled the handle of my gun. They wouldn't separate. He jerked it and the jammed weapons went backwards over his head, flying into the darkness of the studio.

I lashed out in the split second he stared in astonishment at his empty hand. My left fist caught him in the gut of his overalls. My right neatly clipped his jaw. He staggered back, but was no worse off than if he'd lost his balance.

He flared his nostrils and showed his teeth. He was going to kill us both. There was no question in his mind.

"Stop!" said Hitchcock, holding out his scissors.

The big man turned toward him and laughed. "I'll gut you with those," he sneered.

I went for my ankle piece. I had just snapped the strap and was lifting it, when the movement of the man's boot caught my eye. I instinctively crouched and it caught me in the thigh, lifting me off the floor.

I landed hard and the room swirled. I fired. Once. Twice. He reached down and brushed the third shot away, twisting the pistol out of my hand, as the foyer light crashed out. He then picked me up with both hands by the neck, lifting me off the ground like a bag of garbage.

He laughed in my face and I knew he was about to strangle the life out of me, or shake me until my neck broke.

His eyes suddenly widened, however. He flung me back into the umbrella stand and turned on Hitchcock, the scissors sticking out of the small of his back. Hitchcock had scurried into the parlor and fumbled for the light switch and then the phone.

I blinked and concentrated on the pain. If I lost consciousness, I was dead. If I passed out, I'd be split open like a pig.

The big man awkwardly reached behind him and managed to pluck out the scissors. He grinned hellishly and stalked toward Hitchcock, who had just realized that his phone was line had been cut.

Hitchcock grabbed a poker from the fireplace and held it like the kid who's always the last picked and now finds himself at bat with two outs and the bases loaded.

The big man laughed again. "It ain't so funny, now, is it, Mr. Director? You should've let Baby alone!"

The sofa was now all between Hitchcock and the killer. I tried desperately to shake the numbness and get on my feet.

And then the bathroom door opened, and Kim Novak stepped out.

"Hitch?" she said. "What kind of joke is this? I don't have to take this kind of abuse!"

The big man stopped at her voice. He turned. I could see now that at least one of my shots had hit him. The bib of his overalls was bloodstained.

"Stay away from her," said Hitchcock. "You want me!"

But the big man continued to lurch toward the beautiful woman standing in the washroom door, dimly lit by the slanting light from the parlor.

"Baby?" he blinked in bewilderment. "Baby?"

The umbrella stand was heavy, but I somehow managed to crash it once, twice, three times into the back of his head.

I stood over him, barely keeping my balance, waiting for him to rise again.

Kim Novak looked at me. I think she realized for the first time that this wasn't some weird game.

I think I smiled before I passed out. I realized I was in love.

CHAPTER
TWENTY-SEVEN

T hey want me back," I said to Hitchcock. "That's one good thing that came of it." We had just finished a lunch of lamb stew in the kitchen. Alma had made it quite clear that not everyone was invited to eat with the family in the kitchen. In the study, the French doors had been repaired. The afternoon sun was shining gloriously on the Bel Air golf course. The nightmare of a week ago might never have happened.

"And you expected they wouldn't?" He poured me a generous snifter of his expensive cognac. "You're a hero, now, among the studio chiefs for exposing Herman 'Smoky Tex' Grady before the children's show went into production." There was that wicked twinkle in his eye. "The mayor himself now says he should have punched him at the benefit supper a year ago."

"Captain Greene was almost demoted for firing me. As if he hadn't been ordered to do it."

Hitchcock hmmphed. "The nerve!"

"Now you can concentrate on *Vertigo.*" I lifted the snifter. "I think you've ruined me for the cheap stuff." I turned my head gingerly testing my sore neck. My index and middle fingers were taped together to heal the damage done when Cruikshank had twisted away my gun, but at least my face was beginning to return to a normal color.

"I believe we have occasion to share a drink, Mr. Slattery. 'We few, we happy few.'"

"That's Henry the Fifth?"

He smiled. "Sherlock Holmes."

I had just about believed him when he laughed. "Tell me," he asked, more soberly, "are you disturbed by having killed?"

I paused, then said, "I try not to think about it. I can rationalize about the war. In this case, I can think it was either Cruikshank or me and Kim and you. It's better to think of it that way, and, then, not to think of it too much."

"Can one kill without conscience?" mused Hitchcock. "Or must one be mad, as he was?"

"He had his own rationalization, I'll bet. Baby was his prize. Baby had been tainted, had become infected."

"And all of the infected herd must be put down," said Hitchcock.

I sensed what he was really asking. I decided Hitchcock was human. I decided to lie. "One of my pals at the police department said Cruikshank could have killed us all and gone out to dinner with those scissors sticking out of him."

"From a purely physical point of view, a man is hard to kill," said Hitchcock. "The scissors were the only weapon in the house I could think of." He pursed his lips. "Who can imagine? They worked for Grace Kelly."

"An ox like Raymond Cruikshank is guaranteed hard to kill. You've got to hit something vital. If my pop gun hadn't nicked his artery—"

Actually, the coroner was uncertain what had killed Cruikshank. It didn't seem to matter much. Cruikshank had been bleeding internally. My gun. The scissor in the renal artery. It was probably why he mistook Kim for Baby. I had asked if crashing the brass umbrella stand into his skull had killed him. The coroner didn't think so. There didn't appear to be a fracture and his scalp hadn't bled much. The umbrella stand was DOA, however.

"You didn't cause his death," I said. "I did."

"No," said Hitchcock, returning my gesture, "*he* did."

Kim Novak hadn't been there, of course. None of us would ever let out that she had been there. I had been working security for Mr. Hitchcock. There had been an attempted break-in. Raymond Cruikshank, the former fiancé of murder victim Baby Lowen, had been given information by Baby about the houses of wealthy Hollywood. He had burgled several to make up for his failing hog farm in Waterloo (actually Dike), Iowa.

The gang Cruikshank had belonged to had fallen out, and he had killed the other members, except for Smoky Tex, who was gone with the wind. Not even the stolen patrol car had turned up. There's a lot of desert in California and Mexico. More successful in flight than in life, Herman Enoch

Grady had been spotted in Chihuahua, but not apprehended. The citizens of Los Angeles were now safe.

That was the story in the papers.

What we could make of the real story was this. Some years ago, when she was fifteen, Christina Lowen had run away from home with a truck driver picking up a load of pork lips and such to be processed into cheap wieners in Chicago. He kept her for about a month, then she got bored while he was on his trips and left. She modeled for the calendar and learned a bit more about men before she called home.

Her father was furious and would have been more furious if he'd known about the details. He was willing to throw her away, but Raymond Cruikshank made the trip. Cruikshank was about sixteen years older than her, had never had a steady girlfriend, and stammered in her presence. The Chicago police department had an unsolved beating of a pimp about the time Cruikshank went there. A big guy in overalls was the description, but the pimp was still in a coma and who gives a damn about that anyway.

But there was also an interesting missing persons case about three weeks after Christina was brought home. Three wives (one each in Dubuque, Cicero, and Madison) reported their beloved truck-driving husbands missing. Routine bulletins revealed that all three Mrs. Kowalskis shared the same Mr. Kowalski. A couple of live-in girls who hadn't married him turned up, also. The police guessed he had gotten tired of supporting at least three households and eight children and had taken a powder. Hitchcock and I suspected that he had moved on to a reincarnation as a kielbasa.

Christina was grateful to Raymond at first, but the boredom set in. How you gonna keep 'em down on the farm? She introduced him to a few of the things she had learned in Chicago, which kept her entertained for a while, and totally enslaved him. At some point she told Raymond to call her "Baby," and they were announced at the local church to be engaged.

Baby ran away again, this time thinking she had what it takes to be a movie star. Why not? What does it take to be a movie star? They spend so much time pretending to be ordinary people with ordinary lives that ordinary people begin to think they can be movie stars. Just take a look at Kim Novak in a bathrobe or Clark Gable in a uniform and tell me that makes sense.

Your routine sort of man would have cried, got himself a bottle of rotgut, cried some more, cussed the bitch a blue streak, and played "Your Cheatin' Heart" over and over until he was purged. But maybe your routine sort of man never loves enough to go mad. Cruikshank, however, was the sort who let the feelings ferment and ferment in his belly. In the end there isn't much difference in killing a man and killing a hog. They both look you in the eye. They both scream and struggle, desperate to do anything to live just a little longer.

They hadn't heard from Baby for more than a year and a half. Suddenly she calls collect. She needs money. Her father tells her she is dead to him. Cruikshank again rushes to her rescue.

Who knows what happened when he met her? Maybe he was willing to forgive her, and then she laughed at him. Maybe she told him she was pregnant. Killing (we assumed) the truck driver had been revenge. Something else had to snap for him to kill her, then split her like a hog, and toss the carcass behind a bank.

And then he found her autograph book, the bloodstained one we had found in the bib of his overalls. My .18 bullet had nicked the edge of it and that knick might have turned the bullet just enough to guide it towards that artery. She had used the book to keep notes and observations, as well as taking autographs. Her appointments with Leo Ventuno were listed. Once she made a list of what she was expected to do in the smoker flicks and how much each act was worth. It was ugly reading. She also had autographs from Smoky Tex Grady and a young actor under contract to Dumont. Judging from her remarks at the bottom of the page, she had been part of the entertainment for a pretty wild evening. A page or two later, she wrote something vague about "posing" for Walter Lamb. Cruikshank probably read "posing" to be Ventuno's kind of "posing." He read the book as the sordid history of every man who had tainted his Baby, as a list of beasts that needed to be culled.

In "culling the herd," however, Cruikshank had missed quite a few. Walter Lamb, for instance. After a year he turned up in an interview in a small art newspaper published on Long Island. He had been hospitalized for cirrhosis and wouldn't have long to live. He had given up on taking the cure when a "giant ripped open my windows at the sanitarium and dragged me out into the woods." His hospital gown had torn, leaving Cruikshank with a handful of cotton. Somehow Lamb got away in the dark. He stumbled onto a road and ran out in front of an egg truck. The farmer barely missed him, but tossed him in the back and dropped him off in a town Lamb couldn't identify. He hitchhiked to Las Vegas and then east. He sounded in the interview like he wasn't sure whether it had really happened or whether it was an alcoholic nightmare. It made a good story and probably earned him a few of the drinks that ultimately killed him. His paintings supposedly shot up in value for a while after his death.

Errol Flynn knew nothing about Baby. He didn't remember meeting her. He didn't remember signing her autograph book, even though it sounded as if he ought to:

> My lovely,
>> Thank you for making my evening so
>> lovely by coming into my life. I'll never
>> forget you.
>>> Love and kises,
>>> Errol

"Kises?" When Hitchcock telephoned Flynn, Flynn asked him about this Slattery guy he was using for security. There had been two attempted break-ins at his home and if it hadn't been for his dogs—

"I don't think we would have wanted Robin Hood to face Mr. Cruikshank," muttered Hitchcock.

"Cruikshank was crafty in an animal sort of way," I said, sipping the cognac. "He wanted the victims to know he was coming, so he sent pieces of her."

The jar Hitchcock had been sent we stuffed in Cruikshank's pocket. What was I going to do with the jar I had hidden in the bookstore? Maybe it should be reunited with the rest of Baby's body, but sending it to Iowa would cause her father a lot of pain. Maybe I should bury it like a piece of her heart under the Hollywood sign. Maybe it didn't matter. I'd decide later.

"It was the liquid in which one preserves trotters," said Hitchcock. "I recognized it immediately."

"He always waited until his victims were alone. That's why Pete Cohn is still alive, unfortunately. He's always got his thugs with him. As big as Cruikshank was he could creep like a cat."

"Precisely," said Hitchcock. "Alone was what I was counting on."

"So it wasn't a golf ball which broke the French doors?"

"The first time, I found the ball under my desk. The second time there was no ball. On the third occasion, the ball lay on my blotter." He leaned foward. "On the second occasion, no one had been home."

The autograph book had only a few lines in which Baby railed against Hitchcock. It was easy to imagine how Cruikshank had misread it:

> Hitchcock bastard thinks he's too good to mix
> with the xtras after. Tells us what to do then
> gets his flunkies to throw us out. No better
> than anybody else. Gets his and doesn't care.

"I am not a bastard," Hitchcock said on first reading it. "My pedigree is well established."

Neither of us believed Cruikshank had intended to kill Sig Fairfax. Fairfax had somehow escaped mention in the book. Cruikshank had broken into Grady's house through the basement. He'd gone up the servant's stairs from the kitchen. He had either startled Sig hiding in the closet from me, or came up behind him thinking he was Tex.

When had Hitchcock figured out that Raymond Cruikshank was behind it all? He never said. When it was put together, it was, as he said, obvious. Baby had been split like a hog and little pieces pickled. There was obviously some element of passion in the killings. Whenever someone had mentioned a big man, I had thought of Arnie and of that muscle detective with Dixon. When I went down to Venice to find Lamb, Cruikshank had followed me to the phone booth. Why? To find Lamb, probably.

Hitchcock had immediately noticed that the girl at the drug store had mentioned how the big man asking about Ventuno smelled sweaty. Pete Cohn wouldn't have allowed Arnie to smell bad around him. I later confirmed what she hadn't mentioned: the big guy was wearing overalls, not a suit.

And then Edgar Lowen had said Cruikshank was neglecting his farm and that I wouldn't be able to reach him.

"All these details," I said to Hitchcock, "and I hadn't seen it. Some investigator you hired."

"Without you, *Vertigo* may have found itself without a director. I am certain I would have been very disappointed with the direction of whoever they would have hired to replace me. A kiss-kiss ending, no doubt."

He shoved an envelope towards me. There was a check in it. It was very handsome. I could have Pinked for a year and not made that much. "Holy mackerel," I said.

"A certain amount is included for wear and tear."

"It's too much. I did a lousy job."

"It is not," he said firmly, "and you did not."

"Wow," I said. "Thank you. It's enough to make me dizzy. Is that the cognac? Or is that vertigo?"

"As a bonus, I shall keep my trap shut about Mr. Cohn's ill-gotten gains, the ones found in Mr. Ventuno's jacket."

"Thank you," I said. "Pete wouldn't be amused to know I had walked off with his money." I didn't tell Hitchcock that Cohn would especially be ticked with what I had done with it. I had bought a sheet of expensive stationery and a matching envelope, the kind rich people use, and mailed it to Father Domenico, who has a shelter and school in east LA for runaway girls. My unsigned note with the money said that if there were any publicity concerning this donation, there would be no further windfalls of this kind.

"In about a month, shooting will conclude," said Hitchcock, "after which Alma and I intend to vacation in Jamaica. I would like to put my home in your hands. I would like to make you a permanent employee, Mr. Slattery."

"You want me to baby-sit your house? I don't know. Captain Greene wants me back—"

"It's not merely to watch the house. You can be a consultant. And investigate things I might want investigated, perhaps."

"Such as?"

"Whatever interests me. Or you. It will be more entertaining than a policeman's lot. You'd be my personal copper, so to speak."

"I'll give it some thought, Mr. Hitchcock."

"And please, Mr. Slattery," he muttered, "have we not heard the chimes at midnight together, as Falstaff says? All my friends call me 'Hitch.'"

"I should call you 'Hitch.' Is that what you're saying?"

He hmmphed.

I thought for a moment. "Well," I shrugged, "only if you call me 'Chess.'"

His lips curled. "I shall resist the temptation to confuse you with Checkers."

And then he laughed.